EXTINCTION'S EDGE

BOOK SIX

THE FALL OF SAIGON

BY ROBERT LEADER

THROUGH THE HORRORS OF THE
VIETNAM WAR THE TIME TRAVELERS
STRUGGLE TO UNDERSTAND THE
MINDLESS AGGRESSION OF THE
HUMAN RACE. THEY MUST DECIDE
WHETHER THE EARTH SPECIES SHOULD
BE ALLOWED TO LIVE OR TO DIE.

The Marregh/Riken are an aquatic race of amoebic time travellers. Their mother ship is hidden behind the furthest ice planet of the solar system, while an observation vessel orbits unseen high above the only partially inviting world of deep blue oceans.

The oceans are too saline to colonize, but even worse they are divided by dry continents where insane land creatures wage an incomprehensible war.

The first horrified instinct of the Marregh/Riken is to move on, to explore elsewhere in the galaxies, but then they discover an appalling fact. This insane human species stands on the edge of space exploration, already they have begun to explore their own solar system, and eventually they could pose a direct threat to the peaceful races of other star systems.

So the Marregh/Riken begin a systematic study, to try and understand the motives and psychology of these alien creatures, by attaching themselves mentally to some of the key players in the long nightmare which the Earth beings have called the Vietnam War.

The Marregh/Riken must decide whether the human race is fit to survive, or whether they should be destroyed before they can become too powerful and export their blind hatreds out into the galaxies.

The first hosts chosen are the French Paratroop Lieutenant Rene Chauvel, and the orphan child who will eventually be called Phat Sang. Through their eyes the Marregh/Riken follow the events of the lost colonial war.

A brief reminder of Book One
THE LOST COLONIAL WAR

Book One has introduced the Marragh/Riken and their moral dilemma, and is also the story of the last days of French colonial rule and the fall of Dienbienphu, which is seen through the eyes of French Foreign Legion Paratroop Lieutenant Rene Chauvel. It also introduces Phat Sang, the orphan child brought back by Chauvel from the last French patrol to venture out from the doomed French camp. These two major characters, both unwitting hosts to the mind melts of the Marragh/Riken, are the main links threading the whole story together.

Chauvel has survived the Viet Minh prison camps and returned to France. Phat Sangh has found new foster parents who have brought her to the refugee camps at Hanoi. Here another refugee, the ruthless, self-centred Vu Phan Quang, heartlessly steals her rice bowl.

A Brief reminder of Book Two
THE YEARS OF THE WARLORDS

The moral dilemma of the Marragh/Riken continues in a new mind melt with Vu Phan Quang, the corrupt politician first encountered by Phat Sang in the Hanoi refugee camp, as he attempts to escape from the horrors of the communist victory in the north. Quang reaches Saigon and immediately becomes embroiled in the battles of the three rival groups who fought for political control before the USA threw its support behind the South Vietnamese government headed by Ngo Dinh Diem. Rene Chauvel returns to Saigon as a war correspondent for a Paris Newspaper, and Quang becomes captivated by Chauvel's new wife. For Quang wealth and political power are not enough, he craves the ultimate status symbol of a white mistress.

In North Vietnam the hapless Phat Sang and her foster parents endure the new terrors of the Communist Land Reform Campaigns, and again become refugees on the long journey to the south.

A brief reminder of Book Three
BLOOD ON THE YELLOW ROBE

The gentle monk Huong Lin Van becomes the fourth mind melt as the Marragh/Riken struggle to add some understanding of the human spiritual quest to their knowledge of this insane species. But in the madness of Vietnam even the passive Buddhists become drawn into bloody rebellion. Lin Van meets Mary Francis, an idealistic young English volunteer nurse, and the two are drawn together in what can only be a purely platonic friendship. Then Lin Van is injured in a bloody riot, rescued by Mary, and inadvertently breaks his vows by spending the night unconscious in her apartment. He sees fire suicide as his only means of atonement, until an older monk persuades him that his real duty is to toll the bell as their monastery is stormed by Diem's forces. The tolling of the great pagoda bell alerts the world to what is happening to the Buddhists in Vietnam.

The Marragh/Riken are now monitoring the alarming progress of the Earth space race, and a second Timeship arrives with news of a terrible precedent.

A brief reminder of Book Four
THE RISE OF THE VIET CONG

The Marragh/Riken continue to monitor the madness of Vietnam, and now it is the turn of Serhl, the last tri-mind in the observation capsule, to sub-divide and select human hosts. The first choice is Nguyan Nam Kim, a boy taken from his home village, and indoctrinated in the guerrilla camps in the jungles. Nam Kim grows from a hit and run fighter engaging in ambush and night attacks, to a seasoned veteran in one of the groups that merged with the North Vietnamese regiments that eventually marched south to engage in full scale battles with American troops. His final triumph is the initially victorious battle for Hue, the old imperial capital on the Perfume River, which becomes immediately bitter in the awful aftermath, followed by the merciless US counter-attack which drove the Viet Cong out of the city. Nam Kim disappears into the jungle with a handful of survivors, vowing that he will never give up the fight to free Vietnam.

Meanwhile Phat Sang has finally grown up, to become a whore in a Saigon bar.

A brief reminder of Book Five
THE AMERICAN WAR

While Serhl Two has experienced the American war years through the mind of Nguyen Nam Kim, his mind brother Serhl-Three has seen those same war years through the eyes of Irvin Jones, a US Marine, drafted to fight for his country. At one point Jones fights a hand to hand knife battle with Nguyen Nam Kim, a mirror image in which each sees the other as an inhuman monster, which must be exterminated before peace can come to Vietnam.

In a desperate effort to stop an out of control massacre of helpless Vietnamese villagers Jones accidentally fires a shot that kills his commanding officer. Zabrowski, his vicious platoon sergeant is determined to cover the incident up and kill Jones before his tour of duty ends, an opportunity which comes during the battle of Khe San. Zabrowski deliberately leaves Jones and his two friends isolated at the end of a trench line, circling behind them just to make sure they do not escape the attacking Viet Cong.

BOOK SIX

THE FALL OF SAIGON

The long task of alien surveillance continues, through the unsuspecting minds of a handful of participants in the un-folding agony of Vietnam.

Mary Francis has returned to spend a second year as a volunteer nurse in the hospital in Saigon.

Phat Sangh has become a bar girl in a Saigon, and she is Irvin Jones' "Number One Girl." She is carrying Irvin's baby, and when she learns of Irvin's death she naively goes to the American embassy, hoping that the baby in her belly will be her promised passport to America and Irvin's family. She walks into the fire fight as the US Embassy is attacked during the Great Tet Offensive, and is shot in the stomach. She is taken to the Cholon hospital where Mary helps deliver her baby.

Rene Chauvel is ambushed in the street by assassins hired by the ruthless Vu Phan Quang, and is taken to the same hospital. When he is able to discharge himself he goes in search of Quang. Over the years he has tried everything he knows to terminate his wife's affair with Quang, and now there is only one way left. As the battle for Saigon rages on all sides Chauvel seeks a final vengeance on his tormentor.

From their observation capsule hidden in geo-stationary orbit, and from the giant Timeships hidden behind Pluto, the Marragh/Riken continue their tireless task of observing the Vietnam War, and of monitoring every stage of the space race, from the first Russian sputnik to the American Moon Landings. Each step confirms their fears that eventually the human race will be able to export their blind hatreds beyond the confines of their own solar system. Soon they must decide if they can afford to let this insane species continue to advance, or if the human race must be destroyed before it is too late.

The future of the human race is still balanced on extinction's edge.

The corpse of Serhl sank slowly to the floor of the observation chamber, there to deflate into a slowly darkening sprawl of shapeless jelly. The primary tentacles were partially retracted, the soft pink and green coloring fading as though an inner light had gone out. All three of its minds had been abruptly extinguished as Serhl-Three had died with Irvin Jones.

Jarhl and Korhl hovered helpless and stunned. The joint death cry of the lost tri-mind had hit them like a psychic thunderbolt of molten fire, followed by a numbing avalanche of crushing white ice. And then darkness from which they only slowly emerged. They had experienced the instant of dying, the only difference being that now they still existed, while the tri-mind that had been Serhl did not.

The combined thought, of the two Timeships reached out to them on an anguished Revehl/Voronh mind-pulse. The parent ships shared their immediate shock and grief, they communicated spontaneous empathy, but there was also bewilderment and a mind torrent of questioning.

"Serhl-Three stayed too long with the human." Jarhl-One struggled to clarify his own thought and control his own reactions, and was only able to mind-pulse the obvious. "He failed to exit the human mind before the death convulsion destroyed his ability to do so."

"But why? There was no need."

"We know. Jarhl-Three and Korhl-Two have both demonstrated that when a human mind faces imminent decease it is always possible to quickly move to another mind-melt. This knowledge has made it possible for our mind brothers to stay with their human conjunctions throughout the most acute life-threatening situations. Serhl-Three could and should have made such a move into the mind of either Marino or Brown, This is what we expected. But he stayed to solve a mystery."

"The God-concept?"

Jarhl and Korhl were floating together, their trembling bodies rippling against each other. They had to resist the almost human urge to reach down to their lost companion, both with their tentacles and their minds. The catastrophe had happened and could not be reversed. There were no life signals, no mind signals. The end of Serhl had to be accepted. Jarhl concentrated his mind and replied to the Timeship.

"Yes, the odd thing we have discovered in Chauvel, who wants to believe in something, although he cannot define what it is that he wants to believe in. All the human religions, Chauvel believes, are endeavoring to understand and communicate with the same Spiritual Being. The Buddhist faith, as we have seen through the monk Lin Van, believes in the existence of a spiritual plane which is, or can be reached, by Enlightenment. All human consciousness has endlessly reflected this spiritual search for the metaphysical being, or the metaphysical level of eternal existence, to which they hope their vital essence will return."

The Timeships digested and contemplated the thoughts then Revehl qualified/queried: "You refer to that which they term their souls?"

"Yes. Most humans cannot accept the finality of death. They can see and cannot deny the decomposition of their physical remains, but they persist in the belief that somehow their true essence - their souls - can transcend their bodily demise and enter into a metaphysical sphere which is, or is union with, what they call God."

"Irvin Jones shared this belief?"

"Yes. He was confused within his own mind and suffered many doubts, but at the root of his being there was this constant human yearning. The mixture of faith and doubt appears to be the normal human emotional/psychic condition. When death is imminent faith becomes ascendant. It is all they have left. Jones needed to believe. It made his dying easier, almost welcomed. Jones believed that as he separated from this world he would find the heaven he had been promised by his church."

"And Serhl-Three also wanted to experience this transfer into the human metaphysical." The saddened understanding was profound and gentle.

"Yes," Jarhl emitted the mind-pulse equivalent of a deep sigh. "Serhl-Three hoped for some revelation, a glimpse that might confirm or deny the truth of human belief in the millisecond of separation."

"He left his own escape from the dead mind too late?"

"Yes."

"Did he learn the answer to the human mystery?"

"We do not know." It was the most bitter admission of all. "The mind of Irvin Jones and the three minds of Serhl all vanished together. The combined mind shock was a devastating flash of pain. Serhl-One and Serhl-Two had no time to prepare, and the human minds are always a discord of tangled, subconscious impulses. We could not determine whether or not the God-concept truly existed beyond their dying."

There was a long silence from the Timeships. All mind traffic ceased, either in subdued contemplation, or the dulled inertia of grief. The observation capsule hung invisible and alone in its fixed orbit, slowly turning in space with the rotation of the blue, green and white shrouded planet below. From this distance the Earth was infinitely beautiful, peaceful and serene. There were few planets in the entire galaxy which presented such a deceptive countenance. Jarhl and Korhl wondered why they found it so fascinating, when in many ways it was so abhorrent. Now it had taken the life of Serhl, but still they could not feel any malice or hostility toward it. They had always been too involved to share the detached fear of the Timeships.

Revehl re-opened mind communication with another question: "Why was understanding the God-concept given such importance?"

They were not sure themselves, but Jarhl attempted to explain: "We have seen that almost every definitive group on Earth has developed its own religion, or worldview, which argues for some kind of a creation myth, usually with an all-powerful Creation Being, and the concept of some kind of a continuing spiritual world. Our Marregh explorations have also shown that on every inhabited planet throughout the galaxy, wherever there is any form of intelligent life, there are always similar myths and concepts. Even in our own past - before our first sun went supernova - our first ancestors had their own myth of original creation, they believed in the Ocean Spirit of Marre."

"We recall the legend," Revehl's thought was patient but unmoved. But it was discredited when we were forced to leave our first planetary home. The Ocean Spirit of Marre, if it ever existed, was destroyed with the oceans of Marre as the bloated fires of our sun boiled them off into space. No creation spirit saved us, and on all the worlds that we have ever seen there has never been any evidence that any such being has ever saved any of their populations from the folly of wars, or the fate of some natural catastrophe."

"It is so, but even among the Marregh the old legend refuses to die. On Rike it became re-formulated into the concept of a Universal Mind, which caused and sustains all creation. It is a deeply submerged strand of our racial memory, but it persists."

The old ideas had been long abandoned and Revehl and the massed minds of the Timeships were unimpressed, but the lone and ancient thought of Jarehl came through in a now rare flicker of power and excitement that spanned the vast, spatial gulf of distance.

"The Universal Mind was never proved not to exist. Therefore it is still possible that there is something indefinable permeating the known universe. The Marregh/Riken have sensed it as

16

Universal Mind, the human—type species have always sensed it as Universal Spirit — all intelligence senses it, and tries to define it in its own image."

Jarhl was encouraged. He mind-pulsed firmly: "The subconscious belief was very strong in Jones. Serhl-Three sought to look beyond his host's physical existence to determine whether it had any substance. It was an opportunity he/we could not let pass - a risk that had to be taken."

"But there was no substance in the belief." Revehl spearheaded the general consensus again. "There was no revelation, Serhl sacrificed himself in vain."

Jarhl fell silent. Success could have transformed a million years of Marregh thought, but failure resolved nothing.

Below the observation capsule the outline of Indo China blurred and became indistinguishable as the Earth's rotation turned the continent of Asia away from the sun and into darkness. Earth's moon now rose large above them, a blank, white, pock-marked face against the background of far-flung stars. The Earth star was too close and fierce to gaze at directly.

Finally Revehl mind-pulsed again:

"The loss of Serhl distresses you. And you are both weary. Your watch has been the longest we have ever undertaken. We will bring the capsule back to the Timeship. It is time to come home."

"We are to be replaced?"

"The study will be terminated. We have learned enough."

"No," Jarhl and Korhl mind-pulsed in forceful unity. "We do not desire this."

"We have already lost one Marregh tri-mind. The blood feud between Ghauvel and Vu Phan Quang, because of the deep involvement and reluctance to leave of your mind brothers, could bring about another."

"We have learned. The mistake will not be repeated."

"The study serves no further purpose. We have all learned enough."

"Phat Sang is pregnant. Soon she will give birth to a child. We can share in this unique human experience which is so alien to our own means of reproduction."

"We see that you are almost possessed by the mind-melts your mind-brothers have made. We understand your fascination, but to continue the study is dangerous and serves no further purpose. We know that we cannot allow the human species to evolve and menace the galaxy. It is only the method of terminating this menace which remains to be decided."

Jarhl and Korhl boosted the anguished protest coming up from the four Marregh minds on the planet surface, adding their own mind-power to the pleading chorus.

"Let us stay - at least until the means of extinction have been determined. It is our choice. It involves no other Marregh."

"We are all affected when one mind dies."

There was another pause. The Marregh minds became briefly silent. On the far side of the galaxy a rogue comet destroyed an inhabited world. In another quadrant a black hole swallowed entire solar systems. In the centre of the galaxy hot stars blazed in birth with the energy of a thousand Earth suns. Near the root of the neighboring galactic arm a white dwarf star exploded into a brilliant new supernova. Far out in the universe two entire galaxies merged in one stupendous super-collision.

"It is irrelevant." Revehl's thought was softened and resigned. But we will not yet command you to return to the Timeship. Soon your mind brothers must re-enter your bodies so that your natural division process can take place. Already this stage of your development has been long delayed. Then the Earth study must come to an end."

CHAPTER ONE

Phat Sang was now very heavy with her coming child, and her protruding belly was uncomfortably large and had reduced her walk to a slow waddle. She knew that she should go to a clinic and be examined by a doctor, but she had no money, and no husband who could go into debt for her, and so she was afraid that her reception would be a poor one. There were not enough clinics and hospital facilities in Saigon, because all the money that the Americans poured into the city was needed to pay for the war and to keep the politicians rich, and those facilities that did exist were all very busy and might not have time for her. She might even be turned away, and that would be a terrible thing to happen in front of an audience of respectable married ladies. Phat Sang could be stubborn and brave, but she could not be brazen and unashamed, and she preferred to stay away from the clinic.

She was still living with Chin in the small apartment room that the Chinese girl rented in a crumbling building in Cholon. All her savings were gone, but Chin was kind to her and allowed her to continue sleeping on an old mattress on the floor, and also provided her with food. Chin still worked at the *Popeye* bar and made very good money.

With Chin's help Phat Sang had worked out the number of months and days that had passed since she had last seen Irvin. The answer was eight months and fourteen days, and according to a book that Chin had once read the baby should be due to arrive within the next two weeks. Phat Sang was sure that this must be right because the baby had grown so big and she could feel it kicking and moving so vigorously inside her. She was sure that it was going to be a fine and lusty little baby, but she would have to have it alone except for Chin and the old Chinese woman next door who had promised to help, and she hoped that everything would be alright. Old Mrs Long was a cackling busybody, and sometimes Phat Sang did not like the crude jokes she made about her big belly even though she pretended to laugh in order to be polite, but at least Mrs Long had five children of her own, and so she had plenty of experience in these matters.

Sometimes, while Chin was working, Phat Sang would forget the movie magazines that Chin brought home for her to read, and she would simply sit on her mattress with her hands clasped lightly over her belly, waiting to feel the baby move against her fingers. She felt supremely happy then, and she would dream about the baby; what it would look like, whether it would be a boy or a girl, how she would take care of it, what food she would give it to eat, and what clothes she would give it to wear. Perhaps it would have an American face with round eyes and white skin, or perhaps it would be more Vietnamese with narrow eyes and skin the color of pale butterscotch. Those were her happy thoughts. However, sometimes she remembered that the baby would have no father, and that most probably she would have to leave it with cackling Mrs Long for most of the day while she went out to work again to earn more money, and then she was sad.

She had by now almost given up hope that her Number One Number One would return, almost but not quite. She knew from Chin who talked with many Americans at the bar that the Marine Division to which Irvin belonged had been moved north into the Central Highlands, and so she knew that he had not deliberately gone away of his own free will. He had not simply found another girl in another bar, and so there was just a little room for continued hope. However, eight months and fourteen days was such a very long time that by now he must have forgotten her. Phat Sang still dreamed her dreams of her American paradise, and of Irvin Jones proudly presenting her and their baby to Mom and Pop in front of the beautiful little white house on the photograph, but now she knew that they were only dreams. The more practical side of her nature was now prepared to face the future as it had always been, except that she would now have to fight for the survival of the baby as well as for her own.

To help Chin as much as possible and to repay some of her kindness Phat Sang had undertaken to keep their shared room clean and also to do all the shopping and cooking. She went to the market twice each week in the afternoons while Chin was working at the bar, not to the big central market in Saigon, which was too far away and still too dangerous because of the Viet Cong hand grenades, but to a smaller market in Cholon. There she would buy vegetables and rice, and sometimes a skinny chicken, always haggling and bargaining for the lowest price. The morning was the best time to buy the best produce, but the afternoon was the best time to buy cheaply.

Today Chin had told her that she need not go to the market, because her time was near and she could only walk slowly and could not carry too much weight in her basket.

"You should rest," Chin had said. "Tomorrow is my free morning. Then I will go to the market."

"I can go," Phat Sang protested. "We need some rice for tonight. And besides, the shops are all decorated for the Tet festival. It will be pretty to see."

"Alright," said Chin, who was late and did not have time to argue. "But do not try to carry too much."

She smiled and then hurried away, because Madame Chang always scolded girls who were late.

After Chin had gone Phat Sang made the room tidy, and then cooked up a small amount of rice for her lunch. For desert she ate a large orange, for although oranges were expensive Mrs Long insisted that they were good for the baby. She washed up the rice bowl and chopsticks and then rested, and finally she gathered up her straw shopping basket and went out to the market. She wore a white blouse that had belonged to Chin, and a pair of black cotton trousers that could be stretched to hold the shape of her stomach. Her hair was simply but neatly combed, for she could no longer afford the expensive hair-styles that she had favored as a bar girl. She looked at herself in the mirror as she went out, and thought that it would be nice to look pretty and wear her white dresses again.

She had to descend the stairs carefully to the street, but her slow progress did not worry her. She had all afternoon if necessary in which to carry out her little shopping expedition, for there was nothing else to do with her time. If she became tired in the heat then she would go into the courtyard of the little Buddhist pagoda near the market and rest for a while in the shade. The pagoda was her favorite resting place.

It was very hot and the streets of Cholon were very crowded. The people had been saving hard over the past weeks in order to buy new clothes and plenty of rich foods for the New Year feast, and now they thronged the shops to spend their money. The shop windows and the streets were lavishly decorated with lanterns and flower garlands, and paper dragons and paper carps. They reminded Phat Sang that she too would have to buy or make a paper carp to hang in Chin's little room, for then the Household God would be pleased and could use the carp as a steed to carry him up to heaven. The new moon, the first moon of the year, was only two or three nights away, and there was not much time. Already many of the young boys and youths were setting off the noisy Chinese fire-crackers, which sounded like pistol shots all over the city.

Phat Sang wished that she had money to spend in the big shops, but even though she had not she dawdled to look into all the windows. She had already bought the only gift that she could afford, a bright, red silk scarf to give to Chin, which she had paid for with the odd piastres saved here and there by her haggling in the vegetable market.

As she neared the market her attention was distracted from the windows by a noisy procession that was wending its way slowly along the street. A line of five ornate and flower-draped coffins jerked and swayed on the shoulders of their bearers, and all around them the friends and relatives of the deceased were all sobbing noisily. A Vietnamese funeral, like a marriage or a birth, was always a festive affair, and the cortege was swelled by the large number of professional mourners who had been especially hired for the occasion. The mourners followed Chinese tradition and not only sobbed but also banged loudly upon drums and exploded fire-crackers so that their progress was a spectacle and a parade, especially when a number of bereaved families had combined together such as these to share both their grief and the high cost of expenses. There had been a number of such multiple funerals in the recent weeks, and the lines of shoulder-borne coffins entering Saigon and Cholon from the surrounding districts had become a familiar sight. However, most of the people, like Phat Sang, still stopped to watch.

Phat Sang glanced briefly into the worn, yellow and suitably sorrowful face of the man who bore the first corner of the leading coffin, but she did not recognize him, and neither did he recognize her. That was understandable because she remembered nothing of Dienbienphu, and Major Hanh could not be expected to identify the pregnant young woman who watched him pass with the pathetic little bundle wrapped up in white parachute silk which he had taken from a doomed prostitute and handed to another soldier so many years ago. The funeral procession continued on its ostentatious way, and Phat Sang walked on slowly to the market to buy her rice, and a few soya beans, and a small cabbage, which was as much as she could carry.

Later in the evening she had forgotten all about the procession, and while they ate their supper she told Chin instead all about the Tet preparations, and the scene in the pagoda where she had stopped on the way home.

"There were many people there," she explained, after she had swallowed her rice. "And all of them were offering incense and praying to the Buddha. The whole pagoda smelled of incense, and the gongs made sweet music. The monks have hung up paper lanterns and their Buddhist flags, and decorated the altar with fresh flowers, and it is all very pretty."

"Madame Chang let us put up a huge paper dragon," said Chin, who had her own story to tell. "He is red and gold with a long scaly tail and he breathes fire, and we have pinned him to the wall behind the bar."

"I burned an incense stick at the altar and prayed," said Phat Sang. "And a monk said that my baby would be big and healthy."

"I talked with Madame Chang today." Chin was bursting with news. "And she said that if you wish you can come back to the *Popeye* when the baby is born. Madame Chang says that you were very silly, but you were a good bar girl, and because it is Tet and time to forgive she will let you come back."

Phat Sang looked up hopefully, for there were many times when she missed the bar, and the friendly, free-spending Americans, and the companionship of the other girls. There had been times when it had been hard to resist the entreaties of Chin and other well-meaning friends who had urged her to have the baby aborted. Now she was still glad that she had decided to have the baby, because she wanted the baby very much, even though Irvin had failed to return. But the question of her future was a worry. She saw that Chin was serious and she smiled.

"I would like that very much. If I am a bar girl again I can pay Mrs Long to take care of my baby while I am away."

As she spoke the baby kicked inside her womb and made her drop her hands to her belly and wince.

Chin laughed. "I think you are going to have another little bar girl."

Phat Sang laughed also. "No, it will be a boy. He will be a Number One Number One boy, like Irvin."

They gossiped some more, and then because it was past midnight they washed their hands and faces and climbed into their beds and went to sleep.

******

The night curfew lasted from midnight until four am but although nothing moved openly in the streets during those hours except for the police and military patrols, the twin cities of Saigon and Cholon were never silent. The constant flow of jet aircraft that thundered in and out of Tan Son Nhut recognized no curfew, and the heavy bombers that could rattle the windows in their frames did so as much by night as by day. Six miles north of the city behind the suburb of Gia Dinh the Viet Cong frequently made merry with mortars and small artillery pieces, and so a totally quiet night in Saigon was a rare event indeed. Tonight with Tet so close the fire-crackers could be heard banging at intervals throughout the city, and along the dark edges of the seemingly deserted streets a few stealthy figures moved.

Major Hanh had a guide, and the guide was another old friend of Phat Sang's. The gang-leader Suu had proved a valuable recruit to the Viet Cong, and had helped to organize many of the roaming gangs of orphan children into message-carriers and links between the underground seven-man cells. Now, because of his almost unique knowledge of the city's back alleys, and its hiding places and bolt holes, Suu had been promoted to the important task of assisting Major Hanh.

The North Vietnamese Major had the seemingly impossible job of infiltrating not only his own battalion, but also twelve additional battalions of regular Viet Cong guerrillas into the city, but so far they had succeeded without arousing a single wrinkle of suspicion among any of the American or South Vietnamese intelligence services. The men had entered the city in ones or twos, or in whole squads with the funeral processions, and had been effectively hidden away by Suu and the other Viet Cong sympathizers. At least half the population of Saigon and Cholon were National Liberation Front supporters and as yet none of them had betrayed their cause.

Hanh was a part of what was officially known as the 214th Hanoi Unit, which was under the command of a Brigadier-General who had set up his Command Headquarters in a small Buddhist pagoda in Cholon. Other units were to strike at other cities, but the 214th was to attempt the take-over of Saigon.

Suu led the way through short cuts and pitch black alleys until soon they were back at the small cemetery where the funeral procession had ended earlier in the day. Here they had religiously buried the five coffins that had been brought in from the countryside, and they moved like dark shadows towards the fresh graves. The cemetery had been marred by a litter of shanty huts that had grown up over the untended plots because there were so many refugees who had nowhere else to live, and now like the ghosts of the dead arising more dark shapes began to emerge from these night-shrouded hovels. These apparitions were expected, but even so such was the skin-prickling atmosphere of the graveyard that Hanh reached instinctively for the revolver that was tucked into the waistband of his black pajama trousers. Suu smiled a greeting, for he was a young man confident on his own ground, and the murmurs of greeting were returned.

A score of men had gathered, and all of them carried spades. Hanh issued brief orders and six of the men departed like black phantoms to watch the approaches to the cemetery and guard against any surprise by police patrols. The others began to dig swiftly to uncover the first of the new graves. Suu and Hanh stayed alert and watchful, but no one came to disturb them. The refugees in the pitiful shanty huts stayed wisely silent and incurious behind their sacking and cardboard walls and not a chink of light showed.

A cat moved between the small, grey stone stupa spires that marked some of the more important graves, and Hanh swung towards it with one hand again dropping to his revolver. Suu made a soft hissing noise between his teeth and the frightened cat shot away, as though appalled by what it had seen. Suu smiled briefly at his commanding officer, and Hanh smiled briefly in return. Hanh envied the boy his cool nerves and his brash, youthful confidence, but he knew that his own experience was of more value. Beside them the industrious team of grave-robbers had not even paused in their digging.

The earth was soft, and after a few minutes the first of the ornate, brass-plated coffins was uncovered. The long white silk ropes that had been used to lower it to its resting place had been surreptitiously dropped on top of the coffin instead of being drawn away from underneath, and now the coffin was carefully lifted out again on to the surface of the earth. Suu produced a large screwdriver from his waistband and quickly began to unfasten the screws that held down the lid. When he had finished the lid was removed, and inside the coffin were revealed gleaming rows of well-oiled automatic rifles, together with neatly-packed boxes of ammunition clips. The group of diggers reached inside to take out their weapons, and their teeth flashed white in an exchange of satisfied smiles. Hanh smiled too, sharing in their triumph, even though the weight of the coffin had almost broken his shoulder on the way into the city.

The coffin was emptied and then the lid was replaced and it was buried again, and the soil replaced above it as neatly and as reverently as before. Then while some of the men carried bundles of rifles and the boxes of ammunition to the nearest distributing centre those that remained moved on to dig up the next coffin. It was a pattern that had been repeated in all the cemeteries throughout the city on every night over the past few weeks, and it was only one of the methods by which the Viet Cong were smuggling in the weapons needed for the carefully planned Tet Offensive.

CHAPTER TWO

The following evening Phat Sang made a paper carp to hang up for the Household God. With a pencil she drew the long fish shape on to a large sheet of white paper and then she cut it out carefully with a pair of scissors. Then she persuaded the eldest of Mrs Long's five children to let her borrow a box of paints, and she painted in the individual fish scales in bright golden yellow. The fins and the tail she painted crimson red, and the single eye she painted blue with a jet black pupil. It was a very life-like eye, and in fact the carp looked almost as realistic as the ones that could be bought in the shops, and Phat Sang was very pleased with her own efforts. She pinned the carp on to the wall above her magazine pictures of autumn and winter, and waited for Chin to come home from the *Popeye* and admire her handiwork.

It was almost midnight when she heard the downstairs door slam as Chin entered from the street. Phat Sang put down her movie magazine and listened expectantly for the quick patter of Chin's high-heeled shoes on the stairs. Chin always ran up to their room because the stairs were badly lit and she did not like the dark. Tonight Chin climbed the stairs slowly, and Phat Sang had plenty of time to lift her clumsy body to her feet and open the door.

Chin faced her uncertainly, and for a moment Phat Sang did not realize that there was anything wrong. She was too impatient to show off the results of her labors. She held the door open wide and stood back so that Chin could see through to the far wall.

"I have made a carp," she said proudly. "Now the Household God will be pleased, and he will bring us good luck all through the New Year."

Chin did not look at the carp, instead she looked at Phat Sang. Chin wore her white bargirl's dress, cut modestly high over her small breasts but cut to reveal her shapely legs, and she carried a white leather handbag by a strap over one shoulder. She looked very pretty except that her face was clouded with sadness, and her slanted, almond eyes were moist with tears. Phat Sang looked so happy and her news was so bad that Chin put her arms around her friend and began to weep.

"Our luck is not good," she said. "The God is angry and you have put up the carp too late."

Phat Sang did not understand, but Chin's words carried a terrible sense of imminent disaster and she was afraid. Her heart began to pump the frightened blood a little faster in her veins and she began to tremble. She said in a weak voice that barely escaped through her lips:

"What is wrong?"

Chin lifted her head and then looked into her eyes.

"Tonight Tony came into the *Popeye*. You remember Tony? He is the Mafia-American who was Irvin's friend. For a little while he was my Number One before they both went away."

Phat Sang remembered, and now the fear in her belly took shape because she knew what Chin was going to say, with all the dreadful certainty of one to whom tragedy was a continuous shadow she knew.

Chin went on woefully: "Tony has been wounded. He had his arm in a sling and that is why he has been sent back to Saigon. He came in to the bar very late but I was able to talk to him. I asked him about Irvin for you, and he said — he said that Irvin is dead. The Viet Cong killed him at a place called Khe Sanh."

Phat Sang said nothing, because she knew that it was useless to protest or to disbelieve. Chin would not lie to her, and Tony would not lie to Chin. It must be true because such things were always true. The fear drained out of her, just as the happiness had drained out of her a few moments before, and she felt empty except for the weight of her child. Irvin was dead, and her dreams were dead, and not even hope remained. Her mind was numb, and she did not even want to cry, and yet two large tears trickled slowly down her face. One single tear came from each eye, and one was for Irvin Jones, and the other was for herself.

******

While Phat Sang mourned Major Hanh continued his illicit preparations. He had slept throughout the day, and now that it was night and the curfew had clamped down again over the darkened streets it was time for him to work. He had set up his base and distribution centre in the back room of a small flower shop, and now the scent of gun oil mingled with the softer fragrance of gladioli, and orchids and roses. The little Vietnamese who owned the flower shop was standing by the door to keep watch from behind the blind, and to allow entrance to the dark figures which emerged from the street and passed through to the back room. Here Hanh had cleared away the garlands and wreaths of white lilies that had concealed the arms and the ammunition during the day, and he had set up a long trestle table. A single paraffin lamp gave a dim smoky light, which was enough to distinguish the piles of Ak-47 combat rifles, magazine clips, and light mortars and submachine guns which had been laid out as though for a clandestine sale.

Hanh had two helpers behind the table, the two young girls who normally sold flowers in the outer shop, and behind them the wife of the little Vietnamese who owned the shop showed each of their night visitors out by a safe back route. The wife held a one-year-old baby in her arms, because the child had cried and there was no one else to look after it. Now the baby was silent and content, for she had given him her nipple until he slept. Most of the men who moved past her spared a smile for the sleeping baby, and some of them touched it, briefly and gently to bring them luck.

Hanh issued the weapons and instructions.

"Here is your rifle. The girl comrades will give you food and ammunition. We strike when the full moon shines, and your section leaders will name the targets to which you have been assigned. You must take your positions and hold them for forty-eight hours. Then relief will arrive. Remember that your cause is the people. You fight for the national independence of Vietnam, and for freedom from foreign rule. You are Vietnamese, and your heritage is not to be puppets of the Americans. Remember that — and fight well."

The men nodded gravely and each man accepted his combat rifle or his submachine gun and moved along the table. Some were old men, some were middle-aged, but the vast majority were young men, many of them only boys. They were mostly thin and short, and all of them wore dark plaid shirts, which would be their uniform and help them to recognize each other when the time came. The first girl gave each man as many magazine clips as he could stuff into the small black cotton shoulder bag which they all carried, and the second girl gave them a small basic medical kit and a rice ration that would last them for one and a half days. The two girls smiled, the men passed on one by one, touched the baby, and then the older woman let them out into the back alley where they vanished into the pitch blackness.

After two hours there was nothing left of the great pile of weapons except for one stack of nineteen submachine guns that had been set on one side. Hanh gave out the last combat rifle and repeated his set piece for the last time. He was growing tired of his own monotonous monologue but he put as much sincerity and passion into his words as when he had first begun. The eager youth who stood before him smiled briefly and then passed along the table to collect his ammunition and his rice and left through the back door.

Hanh relaxed and thanked the two girl comrades, and then he moved to the North Vietnamese Captain who stood watching with a revolver at his belt. Captain Quynh was his most capable Company Commander, and Hanh had decided to entrust him with the full command of his battalion.

"You already have your instructions," he said. "The radio station must be taken in the first assault. Use a full company. The other companies you can deploy in that area.

Remember that once we launch our attack they will rush in reinforcements from the countryside. We will be given no second chances."

Quynh nodded and said calmly, "One chance will be enough. But I wish I could be as confident of the guerrilla battalions as I am of our own."

Hanh smiled wryly. "Have no fears. This is their city, and South Vietnam is their country, they will fight even more ferociously than our own regular troops. We are only a token force here, and Saigon must be won by the battalions of the National Front for Liberation."

"That is correct," Quynh agreed. He dispelled his doubts and prepared to leave, but one point still puzzled him. He had not expected to be given command of the battalion and he asked curiously:

"And you, Comrade Major? What is your part?"

"I will be needed at the pagoda," Hanh said. "The Brigadier General will need the help of another experienced officer at his headquarters. The National Front leaders have organized things very well indeed, but this coming battle is far beyond anything they have ever planned and carried out alone."

Quynh gazed at him steadily for a moment, and Hanh wondered whether the Captain knew that he was lying. Quynh was a very astute young officer, and conscientious to a fault if such a thing was possible. For a moment Hanh felt old and weary, and he wished that the many repeated bouts of malaria had not shaken and shivered the very marrow out of his bones. However, if Quynh guessed that he was being misled he kept his own counsel, for he had the promise of glory which even though unexpected he had long desired. He smiled confidently.

"May our cause prevail, good luck, Comrade Major Hanh."

They shook hands briefly, and then Quynh departed through the back door. On his way he too paused to touch the dark woolen shawl that covered the baby and his face was serious as though he murmured a silent prayer, for the baby was the future of Vietnam and it was for that which they were all fighting. He went out and was swallowed up by the night.

Hanh found a chair and sat down, and after a few minutes one of the girls brought him a cup of green Vietnamese tea. He thanked her and sipped the tea slowly, and tried to keep back the disturbed cloud of his conscience which loomed over him. He had lost count of the number of times that he had told each fleeting face that passed before him that relief would come if only they could hold out for forty-eight hours, and each time it had been a lie. There would be no relief, and once they had taken their stand they would have to hold out to the bitter end. Many of the Viet Cong had marched for over thirty miles to take part in the battle, but for many of them it would be their last march and their last stand.

The wife had closed and bolted the back door, and now she moved past him with the baby in her arms. She smiled politely and then disappeared up the stairs to return the baby to his cot in the room above. Hanh thought of Quynh almost reverently touching the baby as he left the building, and reflected that even his deputy Commander did not know the truth. There was no real hope that they could win the battle for Saigon. The real purpose of the offensive was to demonstrate to the Americans that nowhere could they be safe in Vietnam, and that they could not hold on to South Vietnam as a power base within their own political sphere. Ironically they were to fight a battle that was already lost in a war that was already won. The Americans had lost the political war because they had never realized that it was the political war which they had to fight. And they had lost the military war because they could not win it, and eventually they would have to face that fact and withdraw. In the meantime the battles would go on, because the politicians who suffered no personal hardships in war were always the last to realize that the issues had been decided. It was always easier to sacrifice men to a lost cause than to accept defeat.

While Hanh brooded there was a faint whisper of movement in the outer shop. The door from the street opened and there was a muffled gasp of alarm and then a soft, reassuring voice. The outer door closed and the bolt was shot into place, and Hanh set down his tea cup and rose expectantly to his feet. Suu entered the back room with a smile on his face, and it was plain to see why he had startled the little shopkeeper. The ex-gang-leader was wearing black leather boots, and the dark green battle shirt and trousers of a soldier in the South Vietnamese Army. He carried a large bundle of additional uniforms which he threw across the trestle table with a flourish.

"It was easy," he announced. "I simply collected them up from a laundry line beside one of the barracks. I could have bought them from the black market, but that would have been against my principles and would have cost me money."

Hanh asked: "How many uniforms?"

"Nineteen shirts and nineteen pairs of trousers, exactly as you ordered, Comrade Major." Suu paused and then added with scarcely concealed guile: "One uniform I am wearing, seventeen are for the special volunteers who will assemble here at curfew tomorrow night, and one is for the section leader who will lead our attack on the American Embassy?"

Hanh blandly ignored the implied question in the younger man's tone. Instead he reached forward to the open neck of Suu's stolen shirt which showed a white V of under-vest as the South Vietnamese wore them and deliberately fastened the top button.

"The shirts will be worn like this," he explained. "Then we will not make the mistake of confusing our own friends with the puppet soldiers of the enemy,"

Suu stood to attention, and signified his understanding with just a brief nod of his head. His chest was thrust out proudly and his eyes flickered for a moment to the nineteen sub-machine guns which still awaited distribution.

"I will issue them tomorrow night," Hanh said. "One of them is yours."

Suu nodded again, he was so eager that Hanh could feel the sharp hooks of guilt twisting their barbs of conscience ever deeper into his soul. It was wrong to exploit this brave youth and his blind enthusiasm, and yet since time immemorial it had always been the way in which things were accomplished. Hanh steeled himself and kept his face blank.

"Is everything ready? Do you bring a message from the pagoda?"

"All is ready," Suu assured him. "No one suspects that the pagoda is our Command

Headquarters, the National Liberation Front battalions are all in position, and the first aid station has been established beneath the grandstand of the Cholon race track."

"Then we have only to wait," Hanh said. "If all goes well, a little less than twenty-four hours."

Suu smiled, and although he remained standing stiff and straight with his shoulders back he looked hesitantly at his superior. Guile had not given him the answer he sought and so now he asked directly:

"Comrade Major, who will be leading the Embassy attack tomorrow?"

Hanh had started to turn away, but now he looked at the young man again. He had intended to keep his decision secret until the last possible moment, but he realized that that moment had come. He could not keep Suu and the others who must follow him in ignorance any longer. He said briefly:

"I shall personally be leading your section."

Suu gazed at him uncertainly.

"You, Major Hanh? But surely we will all die?"

"Do you think that perhaps I am too old to die? Or that I would ask others to die without being prepared to sacrifice my own life?"

"No, no!" Suu protested hastily. But you are a senior officer — your life is more important than mine!"

"This is an important task," Hanh said quietly. "The assault upon the Embassy will be the signal for the general uprising throughout the city. That is why I shall be leading you."

Suu's feelings were a mixture of embarrassment and the realization that a new bond of comradeship had just been formed between them. They were no longer officer and soldier, but martyrs in a shared martyrdom. The boy relaxed and moved over to the table, and for a moment he lifted and casually handled one of the submachine guns.

"I am eighteen years old," he said slowly. "My home has always been the gutter and my food has always been scraps from the refuse bins. I have been a liar and a thief, and a pimp and a bully, because there has never been any alternative for me." He looked towards Hanh and his eyes flashed with sudden passion. "Perhaps after tomorrow there will be alternatives for others like me who still sleep in the Saigon gutters and doorways. That is why I will fight like a tiger and die like a man."

"Perhaps," Hanh repeated the word, but even though he could not destroy the boy's illusions, neither could he put any real optimism in his tone. He gripped Suu's shoulder for a moment, and then said:

"Go now, and return tomorrow night with the other volunteers."

******

After Suu had gone Hanh told the owner of the flower shop to lock up all his doors for the night. There would be no more visitors. The little man did as he was told and then complied with another request for some sheets of paper and an envelope, and then Hanh advised him to retire for what was left of the night. Alone the Vietnamese Major sat behind the table which still bore the uniforms and the submachine guns, and in the dim yellow light of the paraffin lamp he began to write a last letter to his wife and the two little daughters whom he would never see again. Hanh loved his family very dearly, but he had been away from them for such a long time that by now they would be accustomed to living without him. Their grief, he prayed, would swiftly pass.

Hanh knew that Suu was right, and that he was too valuable an officer to waste himself upon a suicide squad, there were more important tasks that he could perform. He knew too that if the senior officers at the pagoda HQ knew of his intentions he would be ordered to resume command of his own battalion, and to leave the Embassy attack to Suu and his volunteers. Hanh knew these things, but still he had made up his mind on his present course of action. He was getting old and weary, and of late it had been more and more difficult to wrestle with his conscience each time that he sent younger men to their deaths; and less heroically he knew that it was only a matter of time anyway before one of his worsening bouts of fever caused him to die uselessly in his bed.

However, the main reason that Hanh was determined to lead the suicide squad was that he was afraid, and he was not afraid of the coming defeat that would turn Saigon into a shambles, but of the victory that was in sight. He was afraid that after all these years of trial and fighting the main mass of the guerrilla fighters in South Vietnam had been duped and betrayed into fighting for the wrong cause. He had become aware that a great many of the rank and file members of the National Front for Liberation fought for a truly national and not necessarily Communist form of independent government, and when the Americans left those patriots would be the first to face the purge that would follow a Communist take-over. Hanh was convinced that the Americans must be beaten, but he could not be sure that the cost in blood would be worth the price in blood that would follow.

Hanh knew that South Vietnam could not hope to escape the land reform campaigns and all the satanic rituals of the sham trials and mass liquidation that had swept in waves of terror over the north, and he knew that it would be those who had merely fought against the corruption of Saigon and the conquering presence of the Americans who would be the first to die. Those who had fought for Communism would ensure that. Hanh knew that the truth could not become apparent to the peasants who had turned guerrilla fighters until after the Americans had been forced to leave the national soil of Vietnam, and then it would be too late.

And Hanh did not want to be alive to witness the disillusionment that those unfortunates had been deceived into bringing down upon their own heads. It was much easier to lead the suicide squad and die than to live with his own fears and doubts for the future.

CHAPTER THREE

Throughout that long, sorrowing night Phat Sang lay awake on her mattress, staring upwards in the pitch darkness to the invisible ceiling of the small room. She could hear the soft, sleep-muffled breathing that came from Chin on the nearby bed and at intervals the sound of an aircraft overhead. Outside the building distant fire crackers banged because it was almost Tet and the celebrations always began at least three days in advance. The sounds barely penetrated into Phat Sang's mind, and she lay motionless with the two tears dried upon her face. Her clasped hands rested upon her belly but even the baby was still. Her thoughts were all of Irvin Jones and the dream, because even though they were both dead she could not dismiss them from her mind.

If there had been light, and if she had slightly twisted her head, she would have been able to see her pictures of the Ohio autumn and winter from where she lay. However, she could see them just as clearly in her mind, for she knew every glossy, sun-kissed golden leaf and blade of grass, and every snow-laden pine branch by heart. She had gazed at them so many times, but now she would never see Ohio, and the pictures would never come to life. She would never sail across the ocean in a big ship that was even larger and more grand than an Emperor's moated palace, and she would never see the Statue of Liberty and the soaring skyscrapers that vanished like ladders to paradise in the clouds. She would never wear a pretty apron decked with flowers and cook Irvin's rice in a gleaming white and silver kitchen with the coffee percolators bubbling and the Ohio sun streaming through the gay curtains. She would never wear a cocktail dress, or drink highballs, or eat salad and steak, or swim in a real swimming pool. She would never now see or do any of those things, and she would not even see Irvin, her Number One Number One, ever again.

All the magic pieces of the wonderful dream filtered again and again through her tormented mind, for even though she had prepared herself to go back to working at the *Popeye* after her baby was born, she had still dared to hope in the deepest and most secret part of herself that one day Irvin would return. She would never have willingly relinquished her dream, however slender the thread on which it hung, but now fate had destroyed it for her. Her eyes remained dry, but somewhere in her heart she was bleeding with large, silent tears.

The blackness all around her began to weaken to a dark grey, and slowly and almost imperceptibly the dawn light began to creep into the small room. The pictures on the walls, the mirror, the cheap dressing table and Chin's bed all began to take slow shape, like intruding ghosts materializing from nothing into shadowy form. The movement of traffic and the sound of early-rising voices began to penetrate from the street and perversely now that there was something to see and hear, Phat Sang closed her eyes. She squeezed them tightly shut, and gradually fell into a shallow and despondent sleep.

After another two hours Chin awoke and yawned lazily. She lay for a few more moments and then reluctantly got out of bed. She looked at the pale and weary face of Phat Sang and guessed that her friend had passed a restless night. Sadly and helplessly Chin shook her head, and then she moved quietly about the normal routine of washing her face and getting dressed and making her bed. This morning she had to go to work early to help clean up the bar, and so she would take her breakfast with the other girls when she arrived at the *Popeye.* She was careful not to wake Phat Sang and when she went out she closed the door very gently behind her.

Phat Sang slept badly through the rest of the morning, and by noon she was again lying with her eyes wide open. It was very hot and she felt sticky and uncomfortable. The heat seemed to affect her much more now that the baby was so near. She could feel the baby moving inside her, and finally she got up from her mattress and made the great effort to wash herself and take off her nightdress and put on her clothes. Then she did not know what to do because she was too miserable to eat, and so she sat down again on the edge of the mattress, and again her woeful thoughts began to circulate in her mind.

After a while she got up and retrieved the photograph that Irvin had given her from its hiding place. She stared down at the smiling faces of Bob and Martha Jones as they posed for the camera outside their white-painted home, almost ten thousand miles away, and she bit her lip. She remembered the other photographs that Irvin had showed her, the old grey dog Scruff lying on the green lawn, and Sister Helen who wore a yellow dress and had long golden hair. Phat Sang had come to know them so well, but now they would never know her. She looked at the photograph again, and tried the words "Mom" and "Pop", whispering them softly to see how they would sound on her own lips. They would have liked her, Irvin had said so, and especially if she had brought them their grandchild. They were grandparents now, or at least nearly grandparents and they would never know. Phat Sang hoped that Sister Helen would one day give them a grandchild, because they looked so friendly and kind and it would be terribly sad if they had no grandchildren at all now that Irvin was dead. Poor Mom and Pop, they would be unhappy too because they had lost their son. And Sister Helen would be unhappy because she had lost her brother. Even the dog Scruff would grieve for his master who would never come home. Phat Sang wished that she could tell them all that at least there would be the baby that Irvin had left behind.

She thought how nice it would be if she could only write to Mom and Pop, just a short letter to tell them about the baby. She turned the photograph over but there was no address on the back, and Irvin had told her that Ohio was a big state that was almost as big as the whole of South Vietnam, and so she did not know where to send such a letter. If only she did know how to address the envelope then she was sure that Mom and Pop would be pleased to learn about Irvin's baby. Perhaps they would even write back and ask her to bring the baby to America, and send her the money to pay for the ticket on the big ship. They would be pleased to see her and welcome her into their home, Irvin had said so, and now the dream was beginning to come alive again and take new shape. If only she could find out the address to write upon the letter, then perhaps she could still go to America.

She thought of Tony. Tony was Irvin's friend, and perhaps he would come into the *Popeye* again and talk to Chin, and perhaps Tony would know the address where she could write to Mom and Pop. It was a slim hope because Chin had said that Tony had been wounded in the arm and that he was on his way home to America. Perhaps Tony had already left Saigon. Phat Sang fretted over her problem, and tried to think of some other and more certain source of the information she needed.

She racked her brains all through the long afternoon, and because it was so desperately important she could not think of an answer. At the same time she became more and more convinced that if only she could write that letter to Mom and Pop in Ohio then everything would be solved. She would tell them that she was Irvin's Number One girl and that he had promised to marry her, and with the photograph he had given her and his baby to prove her claim they could not honorably do anything other than ask her to bring the baby to them in America. She studied the faces of Bob and Martha Jones in every possible light, and because they smiled so warmly, and because Irvin had been their son and had been so gentle with her, she was sure that they must be honorable people. If only Irvin had told her where to write!

The answer finally came to her much later in the evening, when it was too late to go there on that same day. It was so obvious that she wondered why she had not thought of it before.

Every Vietnamese who wanted to make a journey to America first had to go to the American Embassy to get the permission which was called a visa. She would go there too and ask them for help. She knew that Irvin Jones was a marine and that he came from Ohio, and surely that would be enough for the clever people at the Embassy to find out the rest. The Embassy would give her the address she needed, and she would write to Mom and Pop and then they would arrange everything for her. To Phat Sang it all seemed suddenly very simple and easy, and she hugged herself and her plump, near-to-bursting belly in a moment of pure joy. Now that she had thought the matter out successfully she would not allow herself to have any doubts which might undermine her determination to act, and she decided that she would go to the Embassy as soon as it was opened on the following morning. In fact she would get there even before the doors were opened, so that if there were a lot of other people with business at the Embassy she would be the first to go inside.

In the meantime she could only wait impatiently and study the faces of the American Police Sergeant and his wife in the photograph. She practiced the words "Mom" and "Pop" until they sounded natural and familiar, and she believed in the dream as never before. The dream and its promises soared powerfully in her mind like sacred organ music in a cathedral, for the dream had become almost a religion, and she felt that if only she had faith and believed hard enough then the dream must come true.

******

Phat Sang slept more soundly that night, and surprisingly so did the great majority of the citizens of Saigon who had become accustomed over the years to the sounds of gunfire and explosions, and who now confused the battle with what they thought were the cracks and bangs of the Tet fire-crackers. The first, slender, golden crescent of the new moon showed through the clouds soon after midnight to herald the New Year, and Major Hanh led his suicide squad into action at 2.54 a.m. precisely.

Two South Vietnamese Army trucks had been stolen months before and kept in hiding in readiness for this night, and all the death volunteers wore the stolen South Vietnamese Army uniforms and carried forged curfew passes that would smooth their way through any chance inspection. The trucks took them to within striking distance of the giant, six-storey American Embassy off Thong Nhut Boulevard and they were not even challenged.

When the trucks stopped the nineteen men of the suicide squad disembarked and the trucks swiftly vanished again into the night. They would be needed for other tasks. Hanh and his men had their submachine guns at the ready and moved swiftly down the side road towards the back of the Embassy. In the pale light cast by the curved sliver of moon they could see their target outlined clearly against the cloud-banked sky. The Embassy was a massive square block of white concrete which had cost more than two and a half million dollars to build, set in four acres of green lawns and gardens, and with a helicopter landing pad on its flat roof so that the Ambassador did not have to travel through the dangerously hostile streets of Saigon when he ventured outside. Behind its high surrounding walls the Embassy looked like a colossal iced sugar cube, supposedly impregnable with heavily shuttered windows of shatter-proof Plexiglas, and completely dominating this part of central Saigon.

The mortar and rocket teams who had been assigned the task of giving the suicide squad covering fire from hidden positions on the opposite side of the Thong Nhut Boulevard did so dead on time. Hanh had already pulled a grenade from inside his shirt, and Suu and the others had followed his example. As the shells burst against the front of the Embassy Hanh gave the command and the death volunteers sprinted forward. They raced towards the side wall of the Embassy compound and hurled their grenades.   They dropped low as the grenades blasted a gap through the protective wall, and then they were on their feet and running again.

Two steel-helmeted American MPs on guard duty attempted to stop them, but the sub machine guns cut them down. Hanh was the first man through the breach in the wall and he cleared the scattered rubble with one long stride. Suu was close on his heels with the other members of the suicide squad close behind, and they crashed through the lower branches of some ornamental trees and then spread out as they raced across the compound.

Each man kept his finger tight on the trigger and they sprayed bullets carelessly in front of them. More of the Embassy guards rushed to defend their stronghold and in the answering fire men were wounded and the first of the volunteers screamed hoarsely and died. Hanh threw himself flat in a flower bed and rolled neatly on to his back so that he had both hands free above him to change over the magazines on his submachine gun, and the remainder of his men dived for whatever cover they could find in the landscaped gardens. Hanh fitted a full magazine in seconds and again added his own contribution to the battle. The automatic weapons hammered and flashed and drilled the darkness of the night with spurts of flame and noise.

For a few moments they were pinned down, and Hanh knew that they had to penetrate the building quickly. Out here in the open they would soon be mowed down by the rush of reinforcements, and their deaths would have no prestige or propaganda value if they did not get inside the Embassy itself and hold their positions for at least a few hours. The MP guards from the front of the building were now setting up a murderous crossfire from the two sides and sweeping bullets across the lawns.

Hanh reached inside his shirt for another grenade, and in the same moment he heard the rumble of approaching rotor blades. He looked up in the darkness and saw the shadow of an approaching helicopter pass in front of the moon, and realized that the helicopter was coming down towards the landing pad on the Embassy roof. As he watched the floodlights on the roof top burst upwards to guide the whirling machine down. The helicopter was caught in a blaze of yellow lights and Hanh did not even have to give the order. Suu and the other men aimed their submachine guns upwards, most of them lying on their backs with their shoulders against the cropped grass, and filled the sky with a shattering barrage of automatic fire. The helicopter hovered for a moment and then wisely beat its rotors in retreat.

However, the helicopter had momentarily distracted the attention of everyone below, and it gave Hanh his chance. He rolled to his feet and sprang forward, shouting:

"Comrades, follow me!"

He hurled his grenade at the double doors that gave entrance to the rear of the Embassy and they buckled under the blast. Suu was leaping up beside him, his face fanatical, and a second grenade completed the task. The doors fell open, and on the large, round brass plate above the doorway the proud eagle symbol of the United States tilted to one side. Hanh continued his charge and in the same moment a burst of gunfire came from his left and he reeled and crashed into the doorpost. As he slid down the mighty American eagle fell heavily beside him. On the darkened lawns at least five of the death volunteers sprawled lifeless, but Suu and the other survivors ran over Hanh and surged into the Embassy.

The North Vietnamese Major felt stunned, and for a moment he did not understand why he was sitting so stupidly in the doorway without his weapon. Then he became aware that his chest was burning, as though a furnace raged inside him, and the heat was so intense that he could not feel it. It was a white heat that had mercifully destroyed all his nerves and sensitivity with its impact. Only his mind existed now, and his mind was beginning to fade. Hanh realized without any remorse that he was dying.

Suu had thrown himself flat as he crashed into the Embassy, and he slithered across the floor on his chest with his submachine gun held out before him. He came to a stop when his shoulder crashed into a desk and he instantly rolled himself round and began to wriggle back to defend the open doors. His companions had blundered into crouching positions all around him and he heard at least two voices curse that they were wounded. Outside the compound was still full of gun flashes that lit up the darkness like a small scale display of the northern lights, and chips of concrete and woodwork cascaded down from the ricochet scars where the bullets flew from wall to wall. Suu was gritting his teeth and flinching with every nerve, and then he saw Hanh still sitting in the doorway with his back to the wall. He started to crawl forward more rapidly, but then Hanh opened his eyes, and Suu saw that there were at least three bullet holes in the Major's shattered chest.

Hanh saw the boy squirming, towards him and he made a slow, negative movement of his head. He knew that there was no point in Suu getting his head blown off merely to pull a dead man out of the firing line. It was the duty of those who remained to stay alive as long as possible. Suu stopped moving and pressed himself flat, and Hanh gazed steadily into his wide, death-ready eyes.

"Use the desks and filing cabinets as barricades," Hanh said calmly, "and hold out as long as you can. Send some of your men to fight their way up to the upper floors, because the Americans will try again to land helicopter troops on the roof, and you must make them fight for this building floor by floor."

Suu nodded, and he looked as though he was about to cry.

"Sell your life dearly, Comrade," Hanh said.

He lowered his head, and his gaze fell upon the fallen wall plate which lay like a great golden dollar beside him. The word EMBASSY was still clearly readable above the sharp-beaked American eagle, and the words UNITED STATES OF — were still readable below. However, the side of the plate was blackened and soiled, and the word AMERICA and one out-spread wing of the eagle had been obscured. To Hanh the fact that the eagle had been brought low was a sign that they had won: even though they had lost their lives they had won, and surely now the Americans must retreat from the shores of Asia, and leave the fate of Vietnam to the Vietnamese. Hanh was glad that he had lived to see the eagle fall, and equally glad that he would die without witnessing the after pain of all Vietnam under Communist rule. His eyes closed, and the dark, heavy hand of death smoothed over his eyelids, and for Major Hanh the long road that had started in the mists of war before Dienbienphu had at last reached its end.

During the next six savage and bitter hours Suu and his fellow death volunteers held on to their positions on the ground floor of the American Embassy. Dawn came, and then the Americans succeeded in landing ten helicopter loads of tough combat troops on to the roof, and one by one the men of the suicide squad attained their martyrdom. The one-time leader of the gang of homeless and grubby orphan thieves was the very last to die, and by then he was wounded and helpless, his ammunition was spent and his grenades were all thrown. An American diplomat descended from the upper floors with the helicopter troops and shot him dead. It was the last shot fired in the battle for the Embassy.

******

Phat Sang started out on her long walk from Cholon at about the same time that Suu died, but she did not get anywhere near her destination. The Viet Cong had opened their offensive throughout the city, storming the radio station and launching vicious attacks upon the Presidential Palace and a score of other selected targets, but in Cholon there was very little initial resistance. Cholon simply became a Viet Cong suburb overnight as the Communist battalions revealed themselves, and so Phat Sang did not even realize that anything unusual was happening as she emerged on to the street. She had crept out of their room quietly without awakening Chin, because she feared that Chin might cast disconcerting doubts upon her plans.

The Chinese girl was a very good friend, but she did not believe so implicitly in Phat Sang's dream.

It was daylight but there were no people to be seen, and even then Phat Sang did not suspect that all was not normal. She walked as briskly as possible along the pavement, and her mind was busy with rehearsing what she would have to say when she arrived at the Embassy. In her handbag she carried the photograph of Bob and Martha Jones, which with the undeniable bulge in her belly was the evidence she had to prove her case. She was Irvin's Number One girl, and she was sure the people at the Embassy could not turn her away. In the background of her thoughts there were many loud bangs, almost like machine guns, but she ignored them because this was Tet and the Chinese boys always exploded thousands of fire-crackers which sounded exactly like guns. A window smashed over her head and made her jump, and she looked around the street in startled bewilderment. Then she saw a man crouching on the opposite side of the street with a rifle.

Phat Sang had blundered into one of the few fire-fights between the swiftly-moving squads of Viet Cong and a patrolling jeep full of American military policemen. The MPs had dived for cover beneath their vehicle and the exchange of bullets filled the street. Phat Sang tried to run for the nearest doorway, but with her huge, pregnant waistline she was far too slow. The bullets plucked her from her feet and tumbled her over and over in the gutter, and like Irvin Jones, and Major Hanh, and Suu, Phat Sang became just another statistic in the Vietnam war. In a very small way it was an achievement, for although the vast tide of civilian casualties had now swelled to many, many tens of thousands and no longer shocked anyone, at least the daily increasing numbers were still meticulously noticed, and now for the first time in the capitals of Washington and Hanoi someone with a pencil and a slide rule would at least be fleetingly aware that she had existed. A statistic was at least acknowledged.

Each side would blame the other for her death, but whether the fatal bullet had been fired by an American soldier or a Communist Viet Cong was purely academic and irrelevant. Both sides were equally guilty.

Jarehl was dead. His going had been peaceful, a gentle relinquishing of his hold on life and thought as the maintenance of both became too wearisome an effort. It was the normal way of Marregh departure, with Jarehl himself and all the minds that were within reach conditioned and prepared.Revehl and Mirehl floated side by side at the observation window viewing the Milky Way where Jarehl had preferred to spend so many of his last hours. They watched as the small, streamlined casket which contained the shrunken remains of their colleague was shot like a bullet from the Timeship. Its passage was a brief streak of blurred motion and then it was lost, heading toward infinity and the centre of the galaxy. Its journey could end in the gravitational pull of the nearest star, or last for a billion years before it was swallowed up in the swirling star masses of blazing light and energy.

The Timeship was silent, no minds pulsed. When an elder passed there was respect, and some sadness.

"There is no mind to replace him," Mirehl mind-murmured after the long pause.

"There is no need," Revehl answered in somber mood. "He counseled in favor of the humans, but now no mind shares his perception. He was no longer a coordinator as you coordinate the thought streams which have condemned humanity. Jarehl was a mind alone. If there had been a true need — any significant current of thought — then another mind would have accepted the duty to gather and amplify the stream."

Around them the buzz of mental activity was stirring again, gathering in volume now that their conversation had signaled that that the pause of silence was over. Briefly the two elders shared the wishful thought that they had not exchanged views so quickly. Aboard the Timeship all their comfort and well being was automatically catered for. Their bodies simply absorbed all the protein and nutrition replenishment they needed from the life-giving waters around them. They were free to exercise their inquisitive minds almost without distraction. Enduring the constant chatter of the immature tri-minds was virtually their only hardship.

The present flutter was bickering criticism of the latest actions of the two rebellious tri-minds aboard the observation capsule. With long suffering resignation the two elders reflected on the issue.

******

The mind of Korhl-Two had lingered for four long years in the mind of the Buddhist monk Huong Lin Van. Since the end of the Buddhist crisis, and his own release from the government jail, the young priest had totally withdrawn from the secular world; from all political activity, and from any form of suspect activity that might be unfitting for a true follower of the Noble Eightfold Path. He had concentrated his whole being on his prayers, his healing work, and his search for his own Enlightenment.

The Marregh mind had initially been as spell-bound as its host in pursuing the spiritual quest. Korhl-Two had devoured the scriptures through Lin Van's eyes, sifting their doctrines and their wisdom in search of understanding beyond that of the priest. Only slowly had Korhl-Two become disillusioned, as the final truth, the ultimate enlightenment which they both strained their minds to embrace and achieve, remained tantalizingly just beyond their reach.

And then, just as Korhl-Two had begun to get bored, Huong Lin Van had received an unexpected shock. The monk had made one of his regular hospital visits to pray for the sick and was kneeling at the bedside of a man who stank of approaching death and stale urine. Long practice now enabled him to ignore the smells, and the sounds and activities around him, and when he had concluded his prayer he had raised his bowed head and opened his eyes to meet those of the sick man. The man on the bed had reached out a claw-like hand to touch the clasped hands of the monk. Gently Lin Van had taken the weak fingers between his own hands in a gesture of sharing and compassion. No words were spoken, but the anguish in the dying man's eyes was too much. Lin Van had closed his eyes again and moved them away. When he opened them again he was looking through the glass window of the partition door into the next ward.

He knew that Mary Francis had left Vietnam and had believed that she would never return - but the slight, golden-haired figure bending over a patient in the next room was unmistakably that of the English nurse. He had tried to exorcise her memory but all his prayers had been in vain. He had not been able to forget her. The blue of her eyes, the gold of her hair, the warmth of her smile, every beloved contour of her face; they were all so vivid to him as if they had parted only yesterday. And now she was back in Vietnam. Back, here, in the Cholon hospital back into his life.

His mouth had dried, his heart had started to pound, and the familiar tumult of raw emotions had flooded over him. His first impulse had been one of ecstatic joy and his mouth had opened to cry out her name. But then his self-control had struggled to reassert itself. The sound never emerged. He had choked on it and held it back.

Like a man in a slow-motion dream the monk had forced himself to his feet and slowly but deliberately he had backed away. He held the folds of his yellow robe tightly around his body, as though only the robe could protect him against a force more powerful than his own will. He was oblivious to the rows of the sick and dying who stared at his pale and transfixed face, and oblivious to the bewilderment in the lost eyes of the man with whom he had just prayed.

Mary's back was still toward him, but her profile as she half-turned her head to speak to a young Vietnamese doctor who was studying the progress chart at the foot of her patient's bed was exactly as he remembered it, soft, serious and caring. His heart went out to her like an invisible bird that could not be restrained, but his lips stayed silent and his feet continued their leaden steps backward.

Before Mary could look through the glass pane that separated them, Lin Van had retreated to the end of the ward. There he had turned through another door and fled from the hospital.

Korhl-Two had again become fascinated by the powerful surge of human emotions, and he was at last bored by the monk's chosen life of meditation, prayer and devotions. Suddenly the

Marregh felt the irresistible desire to experience the other side of this strange man/woman relationship, and on that impulse he made the simple mind jump from Huong Lin Van to mind-melt with the English nurse.

******

"Should they be reprimanded?" Mirehl's thought was uncertain. "There is no real need and no purpose to it."

Revehl made the Marregh mental equivalent to a human shoulder-shrug. "Jarhl and Korhl have worked hard. Theirs has been the longest period of surveillance we have ever undertaken, and Serhl gave his life and mind for it. We can afford to show them some indulgence. Also we know — as they know — that their time now has a definite limit. The final decision has been taken. "

Mirehl mind-pulsed agreement with the calm benevolence of the vindicated victor. "In a few weeks the Americans have scheduled another nuclear explosion at their underground test site in the Nevada desert. We shall then have the opportunity to juggle their timing to test our own control as we did with their Soviet counterparts. If we are as successful as before then we will know we have the control ability we need to exercise the Tarlus Precedent." He, too, mind-shrugged. "So it will do no harm to permit Jarhl and Korhl to continue watching their human mind-links until then. There are

72

many here who are not averse to discovering how Chauvel and Vu Phan Quang will play out their lives until the end. I think I may even be one of them.

CHAPTER FOUR

After four years the small Government hospital on the edge of Cholon remained unchanged, and Mary Francis had been both shocked and disappointed when she returned for a second year as a volunteer nurse. The Americans had poured so much money into Vietnam that she had expected some improvement during her absence, but there was none. The sanitation was still an offence to the nostrils, and there was still only one lavatory that would occasionally flush when the rusty links of broken chain were pulled. The big black cockroaches still scuttled around the lavatories and bathroom, and the air was still infested with the swarms of flies that thrived in the back alleys. Sometimes it seemed to Mary that the only really healthy native inhabitants of Saigon were the flies.

The hospital still survived on a pitiful shoe-string budget, drastically short of drugs and medicines and equipment due to the lack of any adequate financial support. The doctors and nurses still over-worked a ten or twelve hour day, and the only significant change was in the increased number of patients that overflowed the cramped wards. They were the same thin, hopeless, haunted faces, peering out from the bandaged shells of emaciated bodies, but now many of the patients were also war-wounded with limbs shattered or burned away, as though the ravages of poverty and disease were not enough to bear.

It was now three months since Mary had begun her second tour of duty, but she had made no attempt to contact the Buddhist monk Huong Lin Van. She thought of him often, especially when she saw the yellow robes of other monks in the streets, or performing their social duties here in the hospital, and sometimes she hoped that they might meet again, and sometimes she hoped that they would not.

There was a lingering fondness in her memory and her heart that would have welcomed such a meeting, and yet in her head she knew that it would not be wise. She had received Lin Van's one brief letter and the fact that he had given no return address had indicated that their friendship was politely closed. Her thoughts had often tempted her to visit the Xa Loi pagoda, in the hope that they would meet by chance in the temple courtyards or beside the shrine, but so far she had refrained out of respect for his yellow robe. There was also the fact that hard work and the needs of her patients occupied most of her time.

******

On the morning that the Tet Offensive was launched Mary arrived at the hospital at her usual time, which was eight am. The British team who had helped to run the hospital during her first visit had long since departed, and now the hospital was run by the Vietnamese themselves. However, she had found one familiar face in the Vietnamese nurse Thi Xin, and because they were old friends she was again sharing Thi Xin s small apartment over the coffee shop. Both girls had acquired pedal cycles on which they traveled back and forth between the apartment and the hospital and they arrived together. Their route did not pass near to any of the priority targets selected for the Viet Cong assault, and so they too were unaware that anything unusual was happening. They dismounted and leaned their bicycles against the wall in the yard behind the hospital and paused for a moment to listen to the loud bangs that echoed throughout the city. Thi Xin smiled, and rubbed her fingers over her ears.

"The Tet festival is a time for much noise."

"It sounds as though a revolution is taking place," Mary agreed.

They walked towards the back entrance to the hospital and Thi Xin asked:

"In England do the boys light fire-crackers like this for your Christmas festival?"

Mary smiled and shook her head. "No, not at Christmas, but the boys do light fireworks and big bonfires on November the fifth. The fireworks that leap up and down and sound like machine guns we call jumping jacks, and the others we call bangers. But in England they are not so loud, and most of our fireworks throw out colored lights and stars."

Thi Xin smiled again. "In the East only the noise is important. The Chinese make the fire-crackers and they have to sound like guns exploding." She paused curiously and then asked: "But what is November the fifth? Is it your new year?"

Mary shook her head. "No, it's just a celebration to remember a day when some men tried to blow up all the politicians in London with barrels of gunpowder."

"You mean that blowing up politicians is a good cause for celebration?"

Thi Xin asked the question with a hint of approval in her eye and Mary laughed.

"With some politicians yes, but not all of them. There must be some good politicians, just as there is good and bad in every other walk of life."

"In Vietnam it is difficult to believe," said Thi Xin sadly.

They entered the hospital and went into the small staff room where they left their handbags and capes, and then they became serious again as they entered the children's ward where they normally worked. The departing night nurse exchanged a greeting and an assurance that all was well, except that the lavatory was blocked again. Mary and Thi Xin exchanged groans, but at least it was better than hearing that a patient had died, which happened just as frequently.

The ward had been built to accommodate twenty-four cots containing twenty-four patients, but now it was packed with thirty cots and over seventy patients. The small babies were laid across the cots in rows of four, and the minimum number of patients to each cot was always at least two. On the floor of the ward and in the corridors outside huddled the patient, black-draped mothers and aunts and grandmothers who were responsible for feeding and changing their own dependents, and each morning Mary had to steel herself to face the scene. Always there was at least one child crying, and this morning it was a small boy of three who had both legs encased in white plaster. The stick-like little legs had been broken when an artillery shell had collapsed his mother's hut on top of him during an American sweep in the delta, and had buried him in rubble. The mother squatted on the floor beside the cot, and even though several weeks had passed she was still shell-dazed and bewildered. She insisted on staying by her child even though she was almost incapable of helping him. She did not seem to hear his crying now, and Mary wondered whether she was deaf, although she always seemed to respond when approached.

The two nurses went to the child and Thi Xin sighed as she looked down at the plastic mat on which the child lay with three others.

"He has wet himself," she said. She leaned over the old woman and began to lecture her in Vietnamese, sternly at first, but then with weary resignation.

The old woman struggled up but still seemed unsure of what was wanted, and in the end the two nurses changed the baby and gave the old woman the wet pair of shorts to wash. Then she seemed to understand and showed toothless gums in an uncertain smile. She took the shorts and sorted through the small pile of personal belongings caught up in the black cloth beside her. After a brief search she drew out a plastic bowl and a small packet of soap powder and shuffled off towards the back yard which was always draped with private washing.

The two nurses moved on to make the rounds of their other patients, and Mary wondered if she could ever become accustomed to suffering such as this. Doctor Richard Keller, the American surgeon who was also working here on a volunteer basis, had told her that she must accustom herself to it otherwise she would break up and have to be returned home. However, some of the cases were just too sad. There was the little boy of five who had had one arm blown off at the elbow, and the rest of his body gashed with wounds when a Viet

Cong mine had exploded and killed his playmates. There was a boy of nine who had one poisoned foot swollen to almost three times its normal size where he had stepped on a poisoned bamboo stake, and there was the girl of eight who had been brought in by an American patrol after a helicopter gunner had riddled both her legs with machine gun bullets. The helicopter gunner had mistaken a movement behind a bush for an adult Vietnamese playing a more lethal game of hide and seek. These things Mary could not accept as normal, even though here they were an everyday affair. However, she told herself that she had worked for eighteen months in these conditions without a mental break-up, and so she could survive another year. She would do it because somebody had to do something to help these people. Their long-borne agony was a call too strong to be denied.

******

Mary still asked her eternal question, why? And so far she had found no answer. One morning soon after her return a child who had been particularly badly mangled by a mortar shell had been admitted to her ward. Later Keller had found her sitting alone in the staff room with tears of despair flowing down her cheeks. The American doctor was in the middle of a dash between two patients, but he spared a moment to pour two cups of hot, pale yellow tea from the vacuum flask that was always kept filled, and sat down to face her across the table.

"I know how you feel," he said. "When I first came here it almost broke my heart too. But I'm a surgeon. I had to put my own heart together so that I could go on helping them." He smiled briefly, and then pushed a cup across the table, "This stuff is horrible but drink it anyway."

Mary looked up from the table but ignored the tea. Richard Keller was thirty-five years old, a tall, dedicated man with smooth black hair and deep grey eyes. His face showed signs of strain, and there was a rugged masculinity in the jaw line that was an improvement on being merely handsome. It was the sort of face that would have domesticated wives sighing before their television sets, and cause single girls to smile brightly and strive to look their best. However, Mary liked and respected him because he cared for people, and not because of his good looks.

"I just don't understand it," Mary said. "Why do people have to be so blind, and so stupid, and so cruel to each other? Why do they have to make war instead of living in peace? Why can't they understand that we're all people and we're all the same, that we're all flesh and blood; that we're all men and women and children, and that nationality and religion and politics don't matter? Why don't they realize that the petty divisions they fight over are not important? Why can't they see that it's not worth all the fighting and the killing and the war?"

Keller considered her anger more healthy than her tears and suggested:

"Perhaps it's because they are not perfect."

"But they must have some intelligence. The politicians who lead Governments and declare wars are supposed to be better than the rest of us, they must have some intelligence." Mary pushed a wave of dark golden hair away from her face and went on bitterly: "When they fought World War One the politicians said that it was the war to end all wars, and so millions of people killed each other and destroyed Europe. Then came World War Two and the politicians said that it had to be fought to make the world safe and end all wars again, and so millions more people killed each other and they destroyed Europe again. And now it's Vietnam, and they say it could be the brink of World War Three, and still the politicians are saying that it has to be fought to make the world safe and defend freedom! Why don't they ever learn? Why don't the people ever learn and stop obeying the politicians and the Generals when they order them to fight?"

Keller said quietly: "Perhaps every generation needs its war, just as every young man needs to sow his wild oats, its part of growing up, a part of being young and supremely confident of your own strength and virility. You have to put it all to the test. For the uninitiated there is always a certain amount of glamour in war."

"Glamour!" Mary's blue eyes flashed with disgust. "That child we admitted a few minutes ago looked as though he had been dipped in blood. Those wounds were horrible. Do you call that glamour?"

"I said for the uninitiated," Keller reminded her. "I guess the guy at his physical peak with a carbine in his hands and the best combat training in the world behind him must feel like a young God, or at least that's the way he thinks he's going to feel before he comes out here. We see a different picture."

Keller paused and then went on: "I can't answer you very well, Mary, because I've never given these things a lot of thought. I only know that I'm a doctor and my job is to save lives — even though there are a hell of a lot of other guys out there in the delta and in the highlands making a mockery of my job by killing, and even though I'm making a mockery of their job by patching some of the pieces together again, I still have to save lives. That's my purpose out here, the purpose to which I have devoted my life, and I can't afford to waste any time or thought to the stupidity and irony of the situation as a whole, because that way I may let some of those salvageable cases slip through my fingers."

Mary nodded slowly. "I can understand that. What I can't understand is why the killing and the war have to go on?"

Keller frowned and then said: "I suppose it must be a basic part of man's psychology to fight, in one way or another. Our battle to save lives is just as much a battle as the ones that the marines and the Viet Cong are fighting in the countryside, and maybe ours is even tougher. Everyone has to strive for something; to save lives, to write a novel, to spread peace, or to win a war. Maybe sub-consciously we're trying to be heroes too."

Mary looked doubtful and Keller posed a question:

"Why did you come back here, Mary? You've already done one long spell of nursing in Vietnam, so nobody can say that you haven't done your share to help these people. They're not a personal responsibility of yours, so why did you come back for another year?"

Mary wondered why she had come back, and it was difficult to explain. She said at last:

"I suppose it was the newsreels on television. In England they come on at six o'clock every night, and it seemed that every night there were filmed reports of what was happening in Vietnam. Sometimes it made me so sick and angry that I couldn't eat. There was nothing that I could do to stop it but I knew that I could go back to help some of the people. I was working in a hospital in England then, but the need there wasn't so great. I knew what it was like out here, and I felt that I just had to come back for another year."

Keller nodded as though she had made his point.

"That's it, you had to come back. You couldn't just sit comfortably at home and let it all happen without making some effort to change things, or at least to make them a little better for some people here in this hospital. The instinct to fight is in you too! If you had really wanted the happy, peaceful existence you crave you could have found it. You could have painted flowers or written poetry on a Greek island, or you could have joined a hippy colony on one of the beaches of India where they do nothing but take life easy and talk about peace and love, or you could even have stayed at home. Instead you chose to come here. You had to come back to fight for lives, even though our fight is as pointless as that of those who are doing the killing. The lives we save will still be condemned to the horrors of Vietnam, which means that maybe they would have been better off dead. It's like giving a beggar a coin, it makes you feel good, but if you can't give him something more than that it only means that instead of dying tonight he has to carry on dying slowly tomorrow."

Mary looked into his grey eyes but couldn't read their expression. She said uncertainly:

"You make it all sound meaningless."

"Perhaps it is." Keller shrugged. "But I can't let my mind dwell on that possibility. That's why I'm going to finish this conversation now. I have too many patients to attend."

Mary nodded. "I have too. I must get back to the ward."

They stood up and Keller reached to open the door for her. As she passed him Mary smiled briefly, and there was both sadness and warmth in her smile. She bowed her head almost immediately, but acting on a sudden impulse Keller caught her shoulders and held her firmly. She turned, her blue eyes startled and surprised, and then Keller leaned forward and kissed her deliberately on the mouth. It was so sudden that the kiss was over before Mary could decide whether she wanted to resist or not. As their lips disengaged Keller said wryly:

"I shouldn't have done that, and I promise I won't do it again. It was just to remind you that that there is more to life than just self-sacrifice. You're a young and attractive woman, and maybe you should devote just a little of your time to some of those selfish extras. You have to find a sense of balance to stop yourself from cracking up."

He had smiled at her, and then hurried away towards the operating theatre.

******

Now Mary finished the round of her patients, with Thi Xin beside her, smiling at the children and sometimes chiding the parents, and she wondered whether she did need to find the sense of balance that Keller had suggested. She wished that Huong Lin Van had not been a priest, or at least that the rules of his faith had not made even a platonic friendship impossible. His company occasionally would have perhaps supplied that sense of balance. However, if Huong Lin Van had not been a priest, he would not have been Huong Lin Van, and so it was a wasted mental exercise. She helped Thi Xin to re-fasten the bandages that had worked loose on a frail arm, and then both nurses turned their heads as a plump Vietnamese matron in her early forties entered the ward.

Madame Phuong was the wife of Doctor Phuong, the Vietnamese administrative head of the hospital, and today her normally solemn, round moon little face was troubled.

"Mary and Thi Xin, I have some extra work for you," she said apologetically. "There have been more terrorist attacks in the city and I think we will have a busy morning. Doctor Phuong and Doctor Keller are already operating on an emergency case, and the casualty department is filling up faster than Doctor Huan

can work. One of you will have to help him and
—" she paused and looked even more
apologetic. " — and the lavatory is blocked
again."

Thi Xin made a grimace of her pretty face.

"I will attend to the lavatory," she said.

Mary smiled, she knew that if it had been
Doctor Ton Thu, the second young Vietnamese
intern who was being over-worked in the
casualty department then Thi Xin would have
made a different choice. Ton Thu was a smiling
and sentimental young man to whom Thi Xin
was engaged to be married, whereas the young
Doctor Huan tended to be far more serious and
practical.

"I will help Doctor Huan," Mary said. "But
what is happening in the city?"

"Who knows?" Madame Phuong made a
helpless gesture with her hands. "People say
that the Viet Cong have appeared everywhere,
and that they have attacked the radio station
and the American Embassy, but everything is
confusion. I only know that there has been
much violence, and that we are receiving many
new patients. "

The two nurses stared at her, and their faces
paled with sudden alarm. Mary began to realize
that those jumping jacks which had sounded
like machine guns were in reality distant
machine guns which had been muffled by
intervening streets to sound like spluttering fire-

crackers, and this was their first indication that Saigon had been plunged into what was to be the bloodiest week of its entire, blood-dripping history. They heard more distant bangs which now had the unmistakable sound of rifle shots, and Mary tightened her lips.

"I'll go to Doctor Huan," she repeated.

They separated and she hurried to the casualty reception rooms at the side of the hospital.

******

The Vietnamese intern was surrounded by patients with only one Vietnamese nurse to help him, and he looked up and smiled when Mary arrived, relaxing the severe and unhurried expression which he normally wore with his white coat and spectacles.

"Good morning, "he said politely, and then because his English was limited, "please help."

Mary returned the greeting and the smile, and immediately took over the task of bandaging a small boy who had several large festering sores on his arm which Huan had just cleaned. She did not really like Doctor Huan, for once she had caught him in the act of stitching a long gash in the thigh of a screaming child whom he had tied down in his practical fashion to a table top. There was no anesthetic, Huan explained, and the wound had to be closed, but Mary did not possess the practical Vietnamese indifference to pain, and they had argued furiously until Keller and Doctor Phuong had arrived to smooth things over. Huan was an exceptionally clever young doctor, but he had shown a sense of Asian bewilderment at all the fuss he had caused. Now he and Mary worked together cautiously, and were extra polite to each other.

Mary fastened the last strip of bandage on the small boy's arm and then smiled at him and returned him to his mother and the Vietnamese nurse who was handling the administrative work. Then she turned to help Huan with the next patient in the queue, a man with a bursting ulcer who had to be admitted for surgery. The patients were the familiar line of sick, broken and suffering bodies, of men, women and children. Many of them had been treated less scientifically by the local Chinese doctors before coming to the hospital, and their bodies bore the circular scars and burn marks made by hot cups or bamboo tubes where attempts had been made to force out their evil spirits. To their minds the Government hospital was a desperate last hope, and when they came here they were usually too weak to walk. Mary changed soiled bandages, filled syringes, gave injections and spooned out medicines as the line shuffled forward, working efficiently and with a tight rein on her emotions because that was the only way in which the job could be done. They admitted only the patients who were too ill to stand, because there were no vacant beds. All others were treated, but had to be turned away.

While they worked there was a sudden commotion of voices, and the waiting queue broke apart into two protesting halves. Three young Vietnamese soldiers pushed their way through the gap, and between them they carried the body of a young woman wearing black cotton trousers and a white blouse which they carefully laid out on the floor. They began an altercation with Huan who was annoyed that they had jumped the line, and Mary stared down at the body. The young woman was heavily pregnant, and there was blood all over the waist and the left side of her blouse and at first Mary thought that she was dead. Then the body began to shudder in heaving spasms, and Mary turned abruptly to Huan.

"Doctor, she's still alive."

Huan stopped his argument with the three soldiers and frowned at her. However, Mary was already kneeling by the young woman's side and the frown went unnoticed. Huan knelt with her, examined the patient briefly, and then removed his spectacles and said:

"It is too late, we cannot save her,"

Another violent spasm of movement constricted the bulging stomach of the young woman who lay on the floor, and Mary could not be sure whether or not the dying woman was conscious behind her tightly closed eyes. She looked down at the pale lips and the sweat-soaked face, and then she glared at Huan.

"No, but at least we can save her baby."

Huan hesitated, swinging his spectacles and wondering whether it would be worth the effort, and then he nodded.

"Alright, Miss Mary, go to the operating theatre and see whether Doctor Keller or Doctor Phuong are free."

Mary nodded more briskly and hurried on her errand, and Huan signed to the three young soldiers to lift their burden again. The three soldiers had found the body of Phat Sang lying in the Cholon street after the battle had passed on, and because there was still a flicker of life in her they had brought her here. Now, under Huan's direction, they carried her over to an operating trolley that stood waiting nearby.

CHAPTER FIVE

Rene Chauvel had fallen asleep shortly after midnight, but less than three hours later he was awake again, uncertainly but instinctively wide awake. At first he could not place what was wrong, the bedroom was in darkness and the hotel was in silence, and Suzanne was sleeping peacefully beside him. He listened to the muffled bangs of the fire-crackers that had been exploding all evening in the streets and reminded himself that this was the Tet festival, the new moon had probably been sighted and there was no cause for alarm there. For a few minutes he lay motionless, and then he closed his eyes again and relaxed. There was another distant explosion, louder and less sharp, and this time Chauvel sat upright in the bed.

Suzanne stirred into sleepy protest."Rene, what is wrong?"

"Listen," Chauvel said briefly.

He left the bed and without touching the light switch moved in darkness to the window. He moved the curtain aside to let a dim shaft of moonlight show up the side profile of his naked form and stared out into the street.

"It is only the fire-crackers," Suzanne grumbled. "And you have spoiled my lovely dream. I was at a Roman orgy, and everybody was drunk with wine. Or perhaps it was a Greek orgy, but everyone was speaking in French, and there was this Negro with — "

"That last bang was a mortar shell," Chauvel said irritably. "I know that sound too well. Something is happening out there."

Suzanne became silent and Chauvel distinctly heard more mortar explosions. He turned away from the window, switched on the light and rapidly began to get dressed.

"Where are you going?" Suzanne asked.

"To find out what is happening. It sounds as though Saigon may be under attack. "

Chauvel tucked in his shirt and buckled his belt, and then sat down on the edge of the bed to pull on his boots. Suzanne watched him doubtfully and then sat up behind him and encircled her bare arms around his neck. She kissed his ear and said:

"It may be dangerous, and you will be breaking the curfew. I think you should stay here with me."

Chauvel finished lacing his boots and then turned his head to kiss her properly. As always it was a long, warm kiss and her tongue began to explore between his teeth. She lowered her hands and began to unbuckle his belt again, but Chauvel stopped her.

"You know I have to go, it is my job."

Suzanne pouted her lips to show her displeasure, but there was also concern in her eyes. She lay back on the bed, tempting him with the careless display of her nude body, but Chauvel left the bed to pull on his light bush jacket. He hesitated for a moment and then decided to take the Colt 0.45 automatic that lay in the bedside drawer. He had bought the gun on the black market a month previously after he had discovered that Suzanne had quietly removed the bayonet with which he had threatened to kill her friend Quang, and although he did not normally carry it about with him he sensed that tonight it might be wise to go armed. He dropped the Colt into his jacket pocket and then paused to kiss his wife goodbye.

"Go back to your dreams," he said. "I may be out all night."

"I shall dream about my Negro," Suzanne threatened.

"As long as you only dream, happy orgies."

Chauvel kissed her again, switched off the light, and hurried out. Suzanne listened to his departing steps along the corridor and then turned over on to her side and composed herself to sleep. However, the distant sounds of battle kept her awake.

******

Chauvel had recently acquired a small and very battered Renault car, which he used partly for his job, but mostly for driving Suzanne down to Vung Tau whenever the road was safe to spend their weekends on the white sand beach. The car was parked in the forecourt outside the hotel and Chauvel hurriedly unlocked the door and climbed inside. He started the engine and drove towards the sounds of the disturbance that had broken his sleep, and with his attention fixed on the road ahead he failed to notice that he was being followed.

Two round-faced little Vietnamese on a small Japanese scooter had pulled out on to the road behind him, and the scooter showed no lights.

Chauvel drove with one hand and wound down his side window so that he could hear more clearly, and as he approached the centre of the city he recognized the sound of automatic weapons rattling in the night. There were more mortar explosions and when he reached the turning into Thong Nhut Boulevard he saw a man standing on the corner of the street. The tall, bony figure with his back to the wall was familiar, and as the man turned his head Chauvel identified the American journalist from the Oregon Star. Chauvel braked the Renault to a stop and got out, and then Bill Harvey came to meet him.

"What's happening?" Chauvel asked.

Harvey looked grim. "One thing, the American Embassy is being attacked. I tried to get closer, but there's MPs down there crawling along the pavement and they sent me back. One guy said that the Viet Cong have actually got inside the Embassy, and the MPs are trying to root them out."

Chauvel frowned, and tilted his head to trace the sound of more mortar shell explosions. "It sounds as though they're shelling the President's Palace as well."

"And the radio station, the guy I talked to said that they're hitting all over the city, and they're taking over Cholon. Then he told me to get my stupid ass off the streets and stay off."

"That's good advice," Chauvel agreed. "Are you staying around?"

Harvey nodded. "For a while, I want more facts. This could be big."

"A deal," Chauvel offered. "One man cannot cover all of this. If you are staying here then I will drive down into Cholon and try to find out what is happening there. Afterwards we will compare notes. "

Harvey rubbed the side of his long neck, considering as he tilted his head to one side. Then he nodded.

"Okay, it's a deal. But be careful, Rene, after curfew the police patrols are liable to shoot on sight, and if there is an insurrection then they'11 be extra trigger-happy."

Chauvel smiled. "I'll meet you back at the Continental. Just keep your own head down."

He returned to the Renault and left Harvey crouching and watching from the street corner while he backed away from the main source of violence. He had the bare facts and he doubted that any details would emerge until the battle was over, and so there would be plenty of time to find out what was happening in Cholon. The Embassy attack was a spectacular event, but it could not succeed and therefore it might well be a diversion for something else, and Chauvel was too old to give all his attention to the obvious and ignore what might be happening elsewhere. He reversed his car and then drove away swiftly through the deserted night streets, but again he failed to notice the motor scooter that kept pace a discreet distance behind him. The scooter had stopped when he had stopped, and while he had talked with Harvey the scooter rider and his pillion passenger had quickly wheeled their machine into a side street. Now they were following him again.

Chauvel drove past the central market, and then put his foot down along the long straight road into Cholon. He did not expect to penetrate very far into the Chinese quarter of the city, for if there was anything serious happening then the police would quickly throw up barricades to control the traffic and cordon off any trouble spots. However, he intended to drive as far as possible, and when he did get stopped there would have to be someone there to whom he could show his press card and ask questions.

He kept the side windows open, but the sounds of the fighting that raged around the American Embassy and the President's Palace quickly faded behind him. He could hear more bangs and series of bangs from the streets that now lay ahead, but he could not distinguish whether they were rifle shots or fire-crackers. He tightened his mouth and decided that Tet was an ideal time to start a revolution.

The silent road stretched ahead of him, like a dark river of emptiness cutting through the built-up waist of the double city. Then as he entered Cholon he saw the distant glow of flames beyond his headlights and slackened his speed. The fires loomed up out of the darkness until they were spot-lit in the headlights beam, and he saw that two cars had been over-turned in the centre of the road and set ablaze. There was no sign of life but he guessed that the Viet Cong had decided to set up their own road block. The cold sweat along his back seemed to condense suddenly and settle into his stomach, and he felt far too vulnerable sitting in the Renault. He backed the car quickly and his instinct told him to turn back into Saigon. However, nothing happened, and after a moment he stopped the car and climbed out on to the pavement.

Except for the burning barricade the road was still empty, and the night still seemed to be deserted. Chauvel moved close to the wall and then went cautiously forward. His heart hammered a little faster as he entered the area of light cast by the flickering flames, but both vehicles were burning themselves out and it seemed as though those responsible had either fled the scene or moved on to find new mischief. Chauvel hesitated for a moment, and then moved past the barrier. He still had no facts and so he proceeded warily on foot.

Leaving the car was his mistake, but his mind was concentrated on discovering what lay ahead. He was sure now that there were more rifle shots than fire-crackers exploding in the city, and if the Viet Cong were making a determined effort to take over the whole of the Chinese quarter then Chauvel had to know. Gathering information was his job, and having left Harvey to cover the fighting at the Embassy he felt that he could not back out of his own share of their deal. He had the darkness for cover, although the first light of dawn was turning the sky to grey overhead, and so he kept going. He wasn't sure whether he wanted to bump into a police patrol or not, for although a patrol might be the source of the information he needed they would also turn him back. If they were really annoyed they might ignore his press card and arrest him for breaking the curfew.

He was listening for more shots or mortar explosions from the streets ahead, when suddenly he heard a rush of feet from behind.

They were bare feet on the stone pavement, for the two men from the motor scooter had removed their sandals in order to catch up with him in silence, but he heard the faint, swift patter as the two men closed the final gap. Chauvel pivoted on his left heel in the same moment that his two attackers tried to run him down, and it was only his old paratroop training that saved him. He saw the two knives flashing towards him and automatically lashed out with a straight kick that caught the first of the charging Vietnamese squarely in the crotch. In the same moment his left arm came up in a protective bar across his body, and then swept back to knock aside the plunging knife that was stabbing down at his chest, the knife gashed open his upper arm instead.

The man he had kicked dropped down on to his knees on the pavement, groaning and clutching both hands to his testicles, but the momentum of the second man still carried him forward and the collision knocked Chauvel off balance and back against the wall. The Frenchman reeled sideways to avoid a second lunge from the knife and then tripped and sprawled over a stack of trash cans that rolled noisily along the pavement. For a moment the snarling young man with the knife had his legs entangled in the rolling cans and spilled rubbish, and Chauvel scrambled quickly to his feet. He remembered the Colt 0.45 and groped his hand into his jacket pocket to grasp the butt, and then his assailant rushed at him again. Chauvel thrust the Colt forward, still muffled inside his jacket, and rammed it hard against the man's belly. He saw hate and fear and desperation all written together in the twisted Asian face, and then fresh pain exploded in his own abdomen as the knife struck home a split second before he pulled the trigger. The heavy 0.45 bullet, fired at point blank range literally blasted the young Vietnamese back across the pavement, and because the knife was still gripped fast in his hand it was drawn smoothly free.

Chauvel stayed propped against the wall, and through pain-blurred eyes tried to line up the automatic on the second of his two attackers. The Vietnamese, who had been the pillion passenger on the motor scooter, took one look at his dead companion and fled. Chauvel remained upright for a few seconds longer, and then he fainted away and slid down the wall into a motionless heap.

CHAPTER SIX

When Mary Francis reached the operating theatre it had been cleared and the last patient had been wheeled away. Doctor Phuong had left but Keller was still washing his hands, and behind him another Vietnamese nurse was replacing instruments in a tray. The young Doctor Ton Thu who had been acting as anesthetist was carefully checking over his equipment. Keller looked up as Mary entered, and his grey eyes gave her a weary smile.

"Well, what's wrong now?"

Mary said quietly: "A young woman has just been brought into casualty. Some Vietnamese soldiers found her lying in the street. She's bleeding badly from some bullet wounds and Doctor Huan says she's dying, but she's also pregnant and has started to have her baby."

"Then you'd better wheel her in," Keller said calmly.

Mary nodded and hurried away, only to return a few minutes later wheeling the trolley that bore the body of Phat Sang. The Vietnamese nurse had helped Keller to re-don his green smock and his mask and a clean pair of surgical gloves, and he leaned over the trolley and frowned. He gestured to the table and the two nurses with the help of Ton Thu lifted Phat Sang into position beneath the bright white glare of the overhead light. Ton Thu automatically fitted the oxygen mask over Phat Sang's glistening face, and began to regulate its flow. Keller lowered his mask for a brief moment and turned to Mary.

"Find a mask in the cupboard and then stay to help. I shall need another pair of hands to help support the baby as it appears."

Mary nodded and quickly found a mask and washed her hands. When she came back to the operating table Keller had fixed a blood-drip tube to Phat Sang's right arm, and with a pair of scissors he was snipping away the red-soaked shreds of her trousers and blouse. When the patient was naked three distinct bullet wounds were revealed. All of them were on the left side of the body below the heart, and one had pierced the side of the bulging stomach. The look in Keller's eyes showed that she should have been dead, and yet the respiratory bag attached to the face mask fluttered erratically, the bag only half inflating with each breath. At the same time Phat Sang's whole body quivered and heaved as the baby tried to push its way into the outer world.

"Swab," Keller said, and when the Vietnamese nurse handed it to him from her tray he tried to clean away the blood and staunch its flow. It was pointless to try and extract the three bullets that were lodged somewhere inside the body and he glanced towards Mary and said: "Position the patient's legs."

Mary did so, bending each leg at the knee in the approved position, and she watched the dark, widening shape of the baby's head as it began to emerge. Phat Sang's stomach was thrusting and contracting violently now, and each labor spasm was forcing the blood out of the wound in her side. Keller and Ton Thu both worked desperately to control the bleeding, while Mary reached forward and cupped her hand carefully under the protruding head. The baby's face was clear, wet and wrinkled, and yet strangely and supremely beautiful. There was something wonderful in watching a baby being born, even though the mother was dying. The determined struggle for freedom that defied all opposition was more stirring than any orchestral hymn of praise or battle; and the miracle of life itself held more promise for the future than any priestly oratory from a golden pulpit, or the sacred nebula of dead words in any book of scriptures. Here was beauty emerging from ugliness, and life emerging from death. Here was perhaps the only true immortality, the immortality of continuing Life itself, which defied any individual span. Here perhaps was the only true God. With each agonizing contraction the baby grew larger, an arm appeared, the miniature hand pressed close to the wizened face, and then the shoulders, and then with one excruciating wrench the whole upper half of the tiny body. Mary needed both hands to hold the baby now, and she remembered that she must not pull. She must only support the frail, red-glistening little creature in human form, and allow it to make its own way and its own speed. The coil of the umbilical cord lay loosely around the infant s neck, and she eased it away over the head before it could tighten and cause any risk of strangulation. Keller's eyes flickered towards her and he nodded approval, but Keller had his own tasks and Mary felt that the baby was her sole responsibility.

Phat Sang heaved again and the baby was born. Mary lifted the child clear, and then straightened Phat Sang's right leg and leaned the little red baby against the mother's thigh. With a small piece of gauze she carefully wiped away the moisture from the baby's nostrils and mouth and eyes.

The contractions stopped the moment that the baby had been delivered, and the collapsed body of Phat Sang gradually stopped quivering and lay still on the operating table. The harsh sighing of her breathing behind the oxygen mask faded into silence, and the respiratory bag folded up for the last time. The young Doctor Ton Thu looked at Keller, and Keller moved his shoulders in a resigned shrug. They had both known that the mother's condition was hopeless. The Vietnamese switched off the oxygen flow and removed the mask from Phat Sang's face, and then began to take away the plastic bottle of blood and the drip tube that connected to Phat Sang's arm. Keller turned his attention to the baby.

"It's a girl," Mary said, and her voice was muffled behind her mask. Her normally serene blue eyes were shining with a mixture of joy and horror, a double reaction to the simultaneous death and birth.

Keller smiled briefly behind his mask, for half a victory was better than none, and then he re-arranged the baby over the mother's thigh so that the chest was lower than the rest of the body and any unwanted liquids could drain away through the tiny mouth and nose. The living girl child was still linked to the dead mother, but the afterbirth appeared almost immediately. When it had stopped pulsating Keller tied the cord in two places and then cut it neatly between the knots. The baby now had a separate existence of its own and was breathing without help. Keller nodded permission for Mary to take it away and wash away the smears of blood, and then he turned his back on the operating table and moved to wash his own hands.

Ton Thu and the Vietnamese nurse both looked down sadly at the still body of Phat

Sang for a moment longer, and then Ton Thu politely drew a sheet over her corpse.

Mary washed the baby and then dried and examined it, and then after staring for a moment in amazement she called for Keller.

The American surgeon had removed his gloves and his mask and he came over to the small side table where she worked. Her tone had not carried any urgent note of alarm and so he did not hurry. He said calmly:

"What is it?"

"Look at this!"

Mary turned the new born infant gently on to one side, and they both looked down at the ugly red mark that was burned like a birth mark across the little girl's right hip. Keller leaned closer, and for a few moments he could not believe in the evidence of his own eyes.

"Good God," he said. "It's a bullet scar. The bullet that pierced the mother's stomach must have creased the baby in the womb. Both of them should be dead. This is a medical impossibility!"

"But the baby is alive," Mary said in wonder.

Keller shook his head slowly.

"I still say it's impossible."

And Phat Sang's impossible daughter chose that moment to screw up her tiny face and utter her first, wailing cry.

******

At the same moment another emergency case had been brought into the casualty department and dumped at the feet of the protesting Doctor Huan. The new patient was a white man with fair hair and knife wounds in his arm and stomach, and had been brought in by two white-uniformed policemen in a small jeep.

"This is a civilian hospital," Huan was saying tartly, "for Vietnamese civilians. This man is an American, or a European, he should not have been brought here. He must go to the American hospital."

The two policemen were in no mood to argue, for their duty lay with the city that had erupted overnight into civil war. They were both nervous enough to keep one hand resting on their holstered side arms, and the driver of the jeep said bluntly:

"We found him in the next street, and so we have brought him here. We are busy men and we do not have time to drive him across the city to the American hospital. You must attend to him or take him there yourself."

"I am a busy man too," Huan snapped. He gestured to the waiting crowd of silent patients who surrounded them and demanded:

"Who will attend to these people if I spend my time with patients who can go to the American hospital?"

"It is not our problem," the policeman said stubbornly. "The Viet Cong are everywhere in the city and we must return to the police station. You can do as you please, but there is a dead one in the back of the jeep. The dead one is Vietnamese, perhaps Viet Cong. Where do you want the dead one?"

"I don't want either of them."

Huan was exasperated but the policemen ignored him. They went back to the jeep and began to unload the dead Vietnamese. Huan gritted his teeth, but then knelt beside the wounded white man. He made a brief examination, and then had to admit that the policemen had been right in bringing the man to the nearest hospital, although for the wrong reasons. The man needed immediate surgery if he was to live. A name was needed for the hospital records, and so Huan searched through the breast pockets of the faded bush jacket until he found a press card which identified Rene Chauvel, a correspondent for Paris Soir.

The policemen had laid out the body of the dead Vietnamese on the floor, and the spokesman came back again to Huan.

"This one has a bullet hole in his middle, and we found a knife by his hand. They were both lying on the pavement, and so we know that they had a fight. I think they must have been lying there for several hours before we came along. We must go now, but when there is

110

more time we will come back to make out a full report."

Huan made a helpless gesture with his hands and then the two policemen departed. The young doctor dropped his hands and shook his head and scowled, and then he looked to his nurse. He intended to send her to Keller, but then he remembered that the English nurse had not come back. If he lost a nurse every time he sent a patient to the operating theatre he would finish up working alone and he already had more work than he could handle. He decided to inform Keller himself and reclaim the English nurse at the same time.

The spiritless eyes of the sick and the diseased and the suffering watched him go, and they could do nothing but wait with uncomplaining endurance for him to return.

******

After Chauvel had left her Suzanne had slept badly and because there was no joy in lying in bed alone she got up earlier than usual to take her morning shower. She was luxuriating under the cold jet when a polite knock sounded on the apartment door, and so she quickly switched off the water, dried herself and pulled on a dress as she went to answer it. She expected to find one of the Vietnamese hotel staff with a message, but when she opened the door she recognized the grey hair and thin spectacled face of Bill

Harvey. The tall American was stooped as though he had knocked his head against too many low ceilings, and his ungainly form looked as though it had been only loosely fitted into both his skin and his clothes. Suzanne thought of him sometimes as a tailor's nightmare, but she liked him because he was polite and friendly in the open and honest American fashion. She was getting tired of the Asians who seemed to use politeness and friendly gestures merely as a smooth mask.

"Bonjour," she said brightly. "You are up early?"

"I guess it's a day for early rising," Harvey said. "There's a lot happening. I heard the shower running so I hope I didn't disturb you too much."

Suzanne smiled. "I was nearly finished anyway. Do come in."

She stepped back and Harvey accepted the invitation, hunching his shoulders a fraction lower as he entered the doorway. He smiled almost apologetically and said:

"I really came to see Rene, Suzanne. Did he get back yet?"

"No, have you seen him?"

Harvey nodded. "About five hours ago. The American Embassy got attacked, a suicide squad broke into the ground floor and they've only just cleaned them out. I was trying to get near when Rene came up behind me in his car.

We had a talk and made a deal. The Viet Cong are hitting the whole city and Rene drove off to Cholon to find out what was going on down there. I stayed to cover the Embassy area and we planned to compare notes."

Suzanne frowned and said: "But Rene has not come back."

Her dark-lashed hazel eyes were worried and Harvey felt uncomfortable.

"Don't fret," he advised her. "Rene's a tough baby, and he knows his way around better than most of us. He's probably having a busy time and he won't come back until he's satisfied that he's got the whole picture. When he does come in tell him that I'll be in my room. I've got some urgent reports to write."

"Alright, Bill, I will tell him."

Suzanne nodded her dark head as she spoke and looked forlorn and vulnerable. Harvey lifted her chin with his finger and repeated:

"Don't fret, Rene can take care of himself, but you'd better stay in the hotel until he gets back, because all hell really is breaking loose out there."

Suzanne smiled. "I will be obedient," she promised, although obedience was something she rarely practiced.

Harvey smiled reassuringly, and then apologized because he had to leave her. When he had gone Suzanne finished dressing, and then brushed her hair and made up her face. She made her morning routine last as long as possible in the hope that Rene would return to join her over breakfast, but at last she went down to the hotel dining room alone. As she passed Harvey's door she heard the fast, busy clicking of a typewriter.

Suzanne preferred a French breakfast that was simply coffee and croissants with a small amount of butter and strawberry jam, but usually she enjoyed her meal. This morning she had no appetite, the coffee did not taste right and she merely played with her croissant. She knew that it was silly to worry about Rene, because he was often away for irregular hours and his job had no precise times for clocking on and off, and yet today she was worried. Like the wife of a soldier or a policeman she had learned that it was pointless to worry while her husband was absent at his job, because if she gave way then worrying could become a full-time occupation, but today she felt different. She would laugh at intuition, and yet she knew something was wrong.

She returned to her room and waited. The hours dragged by and to pass the time she tried to read a detective novel by Simenon, who was her favorite author. However, this morning the story was nothing more than a parade of black words across the white pages of the book, and she could not immerse herself into either the characters or the plot. She gave up and put the book away, and by mid-day she was beginning to feel helplessly lost and alone. She waited another hour with no desire to eat another meal and then she remembered that at two o'clock she had a secret appointment with Vu Phan Quang.

Today was one of those rare days when Suzanne did not feel like indulging in any lengthy sexual fun and games, but she also remembered that Quang was an influential member of the Government, and that usually he knew everything that was happening in the city. Perhaps he would be able to tell her what was happening in Cholon, and whether there was any real need to fear for her husband. Suzanne badly needed someone with whom she could talk and unburden her mind, and there was no one else. Just for talk and comfort she might have gone to Harvey, but even Harvey had called briefly to say that he was going out on to the streets again in search of more news. There was only Quang.

Suzanne hesitated, biting her lip, and then she went to the window. The street below was deserted, for most of Saigon's population had deemed this a wise day to stay indoors. Perhaps she should not go. Perhaps Quang would not keep their rendezvous. Perhaps Rene would phone or return. Suzanne was confused but anything would be better than waiting here in this empty room. She decided that she would make a quick visit to Quang's apartment and then hurry back. It would take her less than an hour. She could have phoned, but what she really needed was a reassuring face, and someone whom she could touch and hold, and not just a detached voice over a wire.

Once the decision was made she slipped on her shoes, and gathering up her handbag hurried out of the hotel. Apart from the shortage of traffic and people there was nothing to alarm her and the city seemed quiet. It took her five minutes to find a taxi and one only came by then because she was lucky. She gave the Vietnamese driver the address and then made herself as small a target as possible in the back seat, just in case they ran into a war.

She reached the apartment even more speedily than usual, but without encountering any disturbance. She paid off the driver and then hurried up the stairs away from the street, and let herself into Quang's rooms with the key he had given her long before. Quang was not there, and so she went into the bedroom that was their love nest to sit down on the bed and wait. She looked up at the ceiling mirror, and then at the erotic books and prints, and for the first time ever she felt a little ashamed of herself for being here. The lilac blue drapes were drawn across the window and the room was quiet and dark, and she hoped that Quang would hurry.

It was ten minutes past the hour before she heard his footsteps on the stairs and then she went to meet him. Quang wore a smart brown western suit, with a soft white shirt and a wide red silk tie, and his smooth face was perturbed. The bland oriental smile which normally showed the silver tooth at the side of his mouth was noticeably absent, and he too was in a hurry. He greeted her and kissed her briefly, and then they moved into the bedroom. Quang turned to face her and said:

"I did not expect you to come today."

"I wasn't sure whether you would come either."

Quang finally smiled, because the fact that she was here despite the dangers pleased his ego.

"I am sorry that I am late. There was an emergency meeting of the Government this morning and I had to attend. I have only just got away." He did not find it necessary to mention that he had only stopped here because he was passing anyway, and that in the circumstances he would not otherwise have kept their appointment. Instead he went on: "But I cannot stay long. There is much trouble all over the city, and I must get back to my home. I have to consider Mai Ahn and my sons."

He spoke apologetically but Suzanne understood.

"I know," she said. "I only came because I thought that you would be able to tell me what is happening. Rene went into Cholon this morning looking for news, and he has not come back."

Quang frowned, and it was a genuine frown because her words had cancelled out the satisfying boost that her presence had given to his ego.

"This could be serious," he said. "The Viet Cong have made murderous attacks all over the city. In Cholon, especially in the Chinese quarter, the Government has virtually no control."

"And what is happening now?"

Quang hesitated, and then decided that he was hardly giving away Government secrets.

"Now it is quiet, what you would call, I think, the lull between the storms. The Viet Cong have established themselves, and now there is a pause while the Government mobilizes its forces to drive them out. We have re-called combat units from the countryside, but there will be a little time before they arrive and the real battle starts. President Thieu has declared martial law."

Suzanne put her arms around him and buried her face against his neck. She felt miserable and said:

"Oh, Quang, I'm so worried."

Quang held her and stroked and caressed her gently.

"I am sure your husband will be alright," he murmured.

He turned and inclined his head until his lips touched her throat, and then her cheek and then her lips. Suzanne groaned under the full mouth to mouth kiss and held him more fiercely. She needed comfort and there was only one comfort she knew. She opened her mouth and extended her tongue, and she could feel the answering desire rising in the Vietnamese. By mutual consent they began to move towards the bed, and they were still kissing hard when the telephone rang.

They broke apart and stared at each other, and then Quang moved away to pick up the telephone. He identified himself and listened for a moment, and then glanced meaningly at Suzanne. He said in English:

"No, Madame Chauvel is not here, but I think I know where I can reach her with a message."

Suzanne started to go towards him but he raised a hand and motioned her to stay back and be silent. He listened for a few moments and then said:

"I understand that. I will tell her, thank you for calling."

He hung up and Suzanne said anxiously:

"Was that Rene?"

Quang shook his head and moved to take her in his arms again.

"No, but it was bad news. The call came from an English nurse at the Cholon hospital. Rene was admitted there this morning after he was found in the street with some serious stab wounds. He is alright, they have given him a blood transfusion and stitched up his wounds, but he has only just recovered consciousness. The nurse said that she has just phoned your hotel number but there was no answer. Rene had given her this number as a . possible alternative."

Suzanne looked distraught and said wretchedly:

"I knew something had happened, somehow I just knew it!" She looked pleadingly into his face. "Please, Quang, take me to the hospital. Now!"

Quang was faintly surprised by her concern, and suddenly he realized that despite her infidelity she was truly in love with her husband. For him their affair had always been an extramarital spoonful of sexual cream, an enjoyable diversion but one which he knew would have to take second place to his wife and sons if there was ever any crisis of choice, and yet it was another blow to his ego to find out that Suzanne held an almost identical view of their relationship.

When she had warned him that Chauvel had threatened to kill him, and then shown him the bayonet that she had removed from her husband's reach, Quang had believed that this indicated that he held the highest place in her affections. Now he knew that he had been wrong, and that her first loyalty was to Chauvel. Quang felt illogically annoyed, cheated and deflated, and yet there was a philosophical part of him which reflected that in the circumstances things were working out for the best. He did not want to waste any more time than was necessary before returning to the villa to take care of his family.

He nodded somberly and said:

"Alright, my car is in the street outside. I will drive you to the hospital now."

"Thank you."

Suzanne showed her gratitude with a fleeting kiss, and then hurriedly gathered up her handbag. Quang led the way down to the car and because his back was to her as they descended the narrow stairs his face was thoughtful. He decided that it would not be wise to let her know that it was he who had paid the two thugs to attack her husband. It was better to let them both think that the attackers had been Viet Cong.

CHAPTER SEVEN

Quang stopped his car only momentarily in the narrow street outside the hospital, and then drove away quickly before he could be seen. Suzanne hurried into the narrow reception hall and found the dumpy little Madame Phuong working busily behind the desk. Mary Francis passed in the same moment and Madame Phuong gave her the task of leading Suzanne to Chauvel.

As they walked along the corridor to the wards the squatting relatives who waited within reach of their own sick watched them pass with curious eyes. They were accustomed to the pretty English girl with the wave of coppery gold hair peeking out from beneath her white cap, but the beautiful and smartly dressed Frenchwoman was an unusual rarity. Suzanne brought a faint scent of Paris perfume into their drab lives, but she wrinkled her own nose against the all-pervading smells of ether and sickness and urine. The hospital was already beginning to horrify her, and when they stepped into the overcrowded men's ward her face whitened visibly. So many of the war patients were only half men with bandaged stumps or sightless eyes, and one man suffered from a perforated typhoid ulcer that could be smelled all over the ward. Suzanne had to fight to stop her stomach from heaving, and for a moment the eyes of the two women met.

"I'm sorry," Mary said quietly. "But there was nowhere else that we could put your husband. As soon as possible we'll have him transferred to the American hospital, but the wound in his stomach was quite deep, and Doctor Keller says that it would be dangerous to move him too soon. And of course with the Viet Cong occupying so much of the city we're not even sure that an ambulance could get through. It's best to wait for a couple of days."

Suzanne nodded, and spared a thought to hope that Quang would make a safe return journey into Saigon. Then they walked on down the ward.

Chauvel lay in the bed at the far end by the wall, and had been given a pair of very old and faded blue pajamas. His blonde head identified him easily and his eyes were open. His face was pale beneath its tan, and he did not smile as he watched them approach. Suzanne ran the last few steps and bent to kiss his cheek. She said with relief;

"Oh, Rene, I've been so worried. Are you alright?"

"I will live," Chauvel said tonelessly. "I have eighteen stitches in my arm, but that is nothing. The doctors have also sewn up a knife wound in my belly, but that will heal."

From behind them Mary said, "I will fetch you a chair," and then she walked away.

Suzanne barely noticed that the nurse had gone. She knelt by the bed so that her face was close to Chauvel's and she was conscious of the strain between them. Her eyes showed a new form of concern and she asked anxiously:

"Rene, what is wrong?"

Chauvel closed his eyes. "You were with Quang," he accused bluntly.

"Rene, don't be so jealous." She tried to sound angry. "That is not true."

"I gave Nurse Francis two telephone numbers to try and contact you." Chauvel spoke wearily and did not open his eyes. "One was our hotel room, and the other was Quang's apartment. She told me that she had to phone the second number."

"But I was not there. Quang phoned back again to the hotel, and I had only just come in."

Chauvel refused to open his eyes and Suzanne felt miserable. If he would not look at her she could not convince him, and this was one time when she could not divert his suspicions by simply making love to him. She kissed him again, uncertainly but hopefully. Chauvel made no response, and finally she had to draw back when Mary returned with a chair.

"Thank you," she said.

She sounded so troubled that Mary paused for a moment. She knew how upsetting the ward could be for a stranger, and through the glass pane of the adjacent door there was an even more distressing glimpse of the children's ward where the overcrowding was so much worse. Mary formed a brief smile of sympathy and said:

"Don't worry, Madame Chauvel, you won't have to squat on the floor permanently to take care of him like the Vietnamese women. We can make an exception and feed him and take care of him ourselves until he can be moved. We have to do it for the orphans and the people who have no relatives."

"Thank you," Suzanne said again. She was grateful and conveyed her feeling.

Mary smiled and went back to her work.

Suzanne looked at Chauvel again. He had opened his eyes but their blue depths gave her no encouragement. She reached for his right hand and then said awkwardly:

"What happened to you, Rene?"

"I was attacked by two men." It was the same matter-of-fact voice. "I think they must have followed me."

"You mean they were terrorists?"

"No, they were not Viet Cong. The Viet Cong arm their guerrilla fighters more efficiently with rifles and grenades. These were just a couple of ordinary thugs with knives, and I do not think that they were out to kill just anybody. I think they specifically wanted to kill me."

Suzanne's face paled by another degree and she looked shocked. She said in a strangled voice, "Oh, Rene," and bowed her head. In the same moment her fingers clasped more fiercely around his hand.

Chauvel knew then that she had warned Quang of his threat to resort to murder as a last resort to stop their affair, and he had no more doubts that the two thugs who attacked him had been hired by the Vietnamese. Suzanne knew it too, and she looked so dejected and guilt-stricken that Chauvel began to soften and forgive her. He knew that she had not intended for either of them to be hurt, and that she merely wanted to continue both her marriage and the side pleasures of her affair. He had grown tired of blaming her, for even when he should have hated her he was still in love with her. In her confused misery she needed him now as much as he needed her, and he responded briefly by tightening his hand.

"Don't worry, Suzanne, it will all be alright. The attack failed."

Suzanne lifted her head and nodded feebly, and then leaned forward and kissed him again. It was a tentative, unhappy kiss, and her tears wet his cheek. Chauvel sighed, and then winced at the constricting pain in his stomach. Then he said:

"How did you come here?"

"In a taxi."

Suzanne had drawn back uncertainly when he had winced, and now her moist hazel eyes were briefly downcast. Chauvel knew it was another lie but it was not important.

"I doubt if you will get another taxi," he said. "If there is no one waiting for you then you had better phone the hotel and try to get hold of Bill Harvey. Bill will come out and collect you. When you get back to the Continental you had better stay there until the city is quiet again."

"But I want to come back here tomorrow, to see you."

This time she was sincere, but Chauvel said painfully:

"Suzanne, for once in your life will you do as I tell you. I am in no immediate danger, but you could be killed if you insist on traveling back and forth across the city while there is a war raging. For my peace of mind stay away, please!"

Suzanne saw that he was serious, and at last she made a reluctant nod of her dark head. Then she cried a little and kissed him again. She was completely oblivious to the fact that there were other patients and their relatives watching.

******

Chauvel was very weak, and it was not long before Mary came to his bedside and insisted that he must rest. Suzanne had to leave but she promised that she would call Harvey and then stay at the hotel. Mary led her out and directed her to the telephone, and behind them Chauvel closed his eyes and tried to sleep.

It had been a strenuous day with more than a score of the civilian victims of the scattered street fighting admitted to the hospital, and dozens more treated superficially in the casualty department. Mary felt tired and beaten, and like the rest of the staff had been driving herself at full pressure throughout the day, but still there was no time to stop. While she had been assisting Keller and then Huan during the morning Thi Xin had been swamped by the demands and needs of their tiny patients in the children's ward, and so their daily routine was well behind schedule. Also seven of the newly admitted cases were more children for whom there were no beds, and the two nurses could only shift some of the squatting relatives in order to lay two additional mattresses on the floor.

Working together again Mary and Thi Xin tried to catch up, straightening beds almost at a run, changing dressings, feeding babies, carrying bedpans, giving injections and dispensing pills and measures of cough mixture and soothing words. There was a limit to what they could achieve and many of their patients watched them with tiny eyes that were deep, dull pools of silent agony. It was a day when Mary began to despair.

Two hours passed before the two nurses had earned themselves a space to breathe, and then a chance errand took Mary back through the adjoining men's ward. Chauvel had dozed and rested during the intervening time, and now his eyes were open once more. He called out to her briefly:

"Mademoiselle, did my wife leave safely?"

Mary paused and then turned towards him, and she had to force a professional smile.

"I believe so. I left her by the telephone in the reception hall, and she had gone when I went past again."

"You did not see the car that came to fetch her?"

Mary shook her head.

Chauvel looked into her eyes for a moment and knew that he should not be bothering her with his personal problem. The wave of her hair had slipped loose from under her starched cap and her blue eyes were surrounded by tired lines and showed signs of a deep, inner tension. He thought that such a gentle young face should not age so soon, and wondered where he had seen such eyes before. Then his mind wound back and he remembered the eyes of the French surgeons who had worked themselves almost to the limits of exhaustion and madness in that hideous underground hospital at Dienbienphu. This girl was under the same strain, and he realized that someone had to slow her down. The chair that Suzanne had used was still by his bedside and he moved his right hand in a gesture of invitation.

"You look worn out. Why don't you sit beside me for a moment — just for one minute, sometimes you must stop running and relax your mind, otherwise your mind will break."

Mary hesitated, but she could spare a moment now. She convinced herself that it was the Frenchman who needed help, and someone to talk to him and reassure him now that his wife had gone, and so she smiled and sat down on the chair.

"Just for a minute then," she consented. And then because Keller had given her much the same advice she saw a need to defend herself and added: But I do relax sometimes."

"How do you relax?"

"Oh, sometimes I play tennis, or go to the Vietnamese theatre with one of the Vietnamese nurses. Or sometimes I just read. I brought some copies of Keats and Wordsworth with me from England."

"Ah, yes," Chauvel said, "Your nature poets. You wander lonely as a cloud, but you are a long way from your English daffodils?"

"And you are a long way from France."

"I am a journalist. I had to come here."

"And I am a nurse. I had to come too."They smiled at each other for a moment, and then Mary said reprovingly:"You should be resting, not talking. You're not off the danger list yet."

"I feel fine," Chauvel lied. "And I am only moving my lips. That does not tire me."

"It does, you should lie quietly."

"Then you talk to me. Tell me what is happening outside?"

Mary frowned. "If s hard to say. Everyone is confused and we only get broken pieces of information from some of the patients who keep coming in. The Viet Cong have taken over most of Cholon, and we have heard that they're setting up some kind of rudimentary Communist Government street by street. They're telling the people that Saigon has been liberated and that the Americans have been driven away, and they've even had loudspeaker vans touring some of the streets to proclaim their victory. What will happen when they reach this area, or when the Government start their counterattack I don't know. All that we've heard over the radio is that President Thieu has placed all of Vietnam under martial law."

"Again!" Chauvel grimaced, and then he asked: "Are you afraid?"

Mary considered, and then shook her head.

"I don't think so. I'm only a nurse, and this is a hospital. I don't think the Viet Cong would interfere with us here, and if they do come I don't see why they should cause me any harm."

"I hope you are right," Chauvel said slowly, "although I cannot share your views. Remember that they are fighting a war, and you will be just one of the "interventionists" who are their enemies."

"I'm not part of the war," Mary insisted. "They should be able to understand that."

Chauvel was silent, and she looked around the ward and began to have doubts of her own.

"Although I suppose that all these people had no part in the war either. They just got caught up in the middle. You don't have to be part of it to get hurt, or maimed, or killed." She had started to relax, but now the trend was reversed and her emotions began to build up to a new peak. There was no escape from the smell of the helpless wretch with the burst ulcer, and nowhere that her eyes could avoid the rows of stumped limbs and bandaged wounds, and the baffled desperation began to flow forth: "Why do people have to make war? Surely they can see that it only causes death, and misery, and suffering. War never changes anything, so why does it have to happen?"

It was such an earnest appeal for an answer that Chauvel had to give it some consideration, although he was beginning to feel increasing pain from his wound.

"I think," He said slowly, "that it is because all life is conflict, right from the first struggle to achieve birth to the last struggle to avoid death. And the conflict goes on all through life, because where there is no conflict there is no life. Every novelist knows that he must create conflict for his characters, conflict with each other, or with the elements, or even within themselves, otherwise there is no story and there is nothing to write. So it is with life and there must be evils as well as good, and despair to balance triumph, and hate so that we can distinguish love, otherwise there is nothing to live. Can you accept that?"

Mary looked at him and then nodded.

"I think so."

"Then you must also accept that the ultimate of conflict is war, war is the supreme conflict, the natural end product. Men fight from the first moment they can toddle, and they do not stop until they are too senile to stand. As children they form themselves into gangs and fight with the gangs from the next street, and then as young men they fight with young men from the next town at the local dancehalls to impress their young women, and finally they go to war and fight on an international basis. If conflict is not forced upon them they will seek it. Every young man wants to go to war and become a hero, although first they have to persuade themselves that this is a just and necessary war, as both sides are doing here in Vietnam, and as both sides in any conflict have always done."

Chauvel was making an effort now to keep the inflection of pain out of his voice, but Mary was listening to him closely and digesting his words, and for a moment she had forgotten that he was a sick patient who should be kept quiet. Chauvel smiled up and her and continued:

"And of course, every young woman wants to love a war hero, or become a war nurse. We all have a masochistic streak in our psychology which draws us almost willingly into our wars. We can find rewards in our pains and our tragedies and our self-sacrifices, almost as much as we find them in our pleasures."

Mary frowned and admitted reluctantly:

"Perhaps you're right, perhaps it is nature's instinct to create conflict and war, and human beings, are a part of nature. But why do the politicians and the Generals have to take advantage of those instincts? They're not blind young men intent on proving themselves, they've lived long enough to know better. They know that the cost always exceeds the gain, and the innocent always suffer the worst hurt. So why do they have to exploit the mass psychology. In England they advertise for recruits into the Army and other services, and it's always the same theme; be a *man* in today's Army, be a leader of men, be a *man* among men. It's all an insinuation that if they don't join the Army and carry guns and kill to order then they are *not men*, and so they get them into the Army and discipline them, and demand blind obedience to orders, and turn them into legal murderers. It's all a wicked exploitation of mass psychology."

Chauvel smiled feebly. "That is true. And the answer to your question of why do they do it is that politicians and Generals are also bound to the laws of conflict, except that their conflict is for World Power. However, when you accuse our western leaders of exploiting mass psychology you must remember that they are only children learning the basic principles when they are compared to the Communists. There is nothing more ruthless and complete and terrifying than the way in which the Communists have exploited the mass psychology of the Asian peasants."

Mary said gloomily: "Sometimes I think that the Communists are easier to understand. Communism exploits the simple peasant people who live simple lives and who can believe in simple basic promises. But the Americans are different, their young men are intelligent and better educated, why are they so easily exploited?"

Chauvel was feeling too weak to concentrate any further, but Mary was still deep in thought and went on after a moment to answer her own question.

"I remember watching a film once," she said slowly and seemingly irrelevantly. "It was an old film shown on television, and it had John Wayne looking almost young. It was called "Fort Apache" or "Fort Something". It was the usual sort of cowboy film, and John Wayne was a Cavalry Captain who arranged a peace talk with the Indians. But the Colonel commanding the fort wouldn't talk to the Indians except to order them back to the reservation. He said it was beneath the dignity of the US Government to discuss terms. Of course there was a war, and the Colonel and most of his men got killed, and the film ended with John Wayne giving a sort of starry-eyed requiem and saying something about what heroes they all were, and how the spirit and glory of the American Cavalry would live on for ever."

Mary paused for a moment, gazing vacantly at the wall, and then finished:

"Sometimes I think the Americans have seen too many of their own Hollywood movies. They've all got a cowboy mentality and they're all trying to be John Wayne. They've blinded themselves with their own Hollywood image and the American dream. To them the Viet Cong are just another tribe of Indians who have broken out of another reservation, and because they are the Cavalry they've convinced themselves that it must all work out right in the end."

"You are too hard on them," Chauvel protested faintly. "The Americans are only in this mess which is Vietnam because they failed to recognize the difference between a Communist take-over of an unwilling people, and a genuine nationalist movement under Communist leadership. The fault is all with the French who left the Vietnamese no road from Colonialism except Communism."

Mary looked down at him, and reverted back to her original trend of thought.

"Do you think there will ever be any end to wars?"

Chauvel made a slow, negative roll of his head, and then gazed back into her eyes. He noticed that they were blue, like searching mirrors of his own.

"No," he said firmly. "We have already agreed that war is the ultimate of conflict which is life. But perhaps they can be limited. The psychological exploitation by the politicians and Generals can be challenged, and perhaps we can win away some of the soldier pawns on whom they rely to fight their battles. Some young Americans have already realized that they are responsible first to their own conscience, and not to any politician's call to duty, and they have refused to be drafted into this war. Wars will continue to flare upon this planet until eternity, but win away some of its raw human material and some of its effects must be reduced."

"And I suppose that to do that is another form of conflict." Mary smiled wryly, and then suddenly she realized that talking had exhausted him and that his eyes had closed. She was angry with herself and said sharply:

"I'm a fool. I forgot that you should be resting."

She stood up and straightened his pillow to make him more comfortable but then hesitated before she left him.

"I should have known better than to let you tire yourself out — but thank you anyway."

Chauvel did not open his eyes, but his lips formed a faint smile. "Mademoiselle," he said politely, "please don't mention it."

Mary smiled at the quaint English phrase, which the English rarely used, and then remembered that she had left Thi Xin to cope alone. Chauvel heard her hurry away, and hoped that at least he had given her some food for thought which would occupy her mind and leave less room for despair. Then he felt his consciousness slipping quietly and painlessly away.

CHAPTER EIGHT

At seven o'clock that evening, an hour over their usual time, Mary and Thi Xin finished their long day's work. It was then dusk and that part of the city around the hospital was relatively quiet and as yet the streets through which they had to ride their bicycles to regain their apartment had not been contested by the Viet Cong. There was nowhere for them to stay at the hospital and so reluctantly Doctor Phuong allowed them to go home. He was a plump little man, a perfect match for his wife, and he warned them to pedal swiftly because the Government curfew had been extended to cover thirteen hours between seven p.m. and eight o'clock in the morning.

The two nurses did as they were told and rode as quickly as possible with their capes flying. Usually the streets were rivers of noise through which the thousands of Japanese scooters and motor cycles darted like silvery flying fish, but tonight they were gloomy and empty. Saigon had become a ghost city, and the poisonous exhaust fumes that had killed off all the rhododendrons that had once flowered along the main boulevards had now been replaced by the more ominous smell of smoke and burning which lingered faintly in the air. The two girls cycled side by side, although Mary could have pulled ahead, she rode a man's cycle with slightly larger wheels, and after tennis cycling was her favorite form of exercise. It was an uneventful ride, although the threat of danger was always present, and they were both relieved when at last they braked to a stop before the coffee shop below their apartment. They wheeled their bicycles into the narrow passageway beside the shop and then hurried up the stairs to the safety of their rooms. They were both breathless, and Thi Xin was trembling.

The two girls showered and changed their clothes, and then Thi Xin prepared a meal. The Vietnamese girl was an excellent cook and enjoyed creating her own national dishes, but tonight she showed no enthusiasm. She made a simple meal of rice and vegetables, and then only toyed with her food when they sat down to eat. The silence was depressing and Mary tried to draw her friend's fears into the open.

"Are you afraid that the Viet Cong will capture the whole city?" she asked quietly.

Thi Xin looked at her with dark, troubled eyes.

"No it is not that. But the Viet Cong have not only attacked Saigon, they have attacked all our cities. They have attacked Bien Hoa."

Mary understood, for the nearby city of Bien Hoa was Thi Xin's family home. Mary had been there several times as Thi Xin's guest to meet the Vietnamese girl's parents. They were an elderly couple living in retirement in a small, neat home that had a miniature patio outside, and in the main living room a small family shrine that bore the framed portraits of their own parents and grandparents. Close by there hung another framed portrait of Thi Xin's elder brother who was a soldier in the South Vietnamese Army. The old couple had been courteous hosts, and had showed pride in both their children. Only recently they had given a modest celebration, which Mary had been invited to attend, after the father of the young Doctor Ton Thu had paid his respects to the mother of Thi Xin in order to arrange the marriage of their children. That had been a particularly joyous day for Thi Xin, but now she said unhappily:

"If the Viet Cong have been so successful in Saigon then surely they must have achieved even greater success in a little city like Bien Hoa. I fear very much for my parents."

"They will be safe," Mary said, although her voice expressed more hope than conviction. "Even the Viet Cong don't kill civilians unnecessarily."

"But my brother is a soldier," Thi Xin reminded her. "That means that my parents will not be treated as ordinary civilians but as a family who support the Government."

"Your parents could hide the picture of your brother in his uniform," Mary suggested.

"Then if the Viet Cong break into their home they will not know."

"The Viet Cong know everything," Thi Xin said gloomily. "The Viet Cong are still Vietnamese, and they have brothers, and cousins, and relatives everywhere. And even if this was not so, my father would never hide my brother's picture." She paused and then added: "I fear for my brother also."

There was nothing that Mary could say, for words were only a minimum of comfort, and after a few more minutes she got up and washed the dishes. Afterwards, while they sipped cups of green Vietnamese tea, she tried to change the subject.

"There was a baby born in the operating theatre this morning, have you seen it yet? It was a little girl with a bullet scar on her hip. The bullets killed the mother, and Doctor Keller said it was a miracle that the baby lived,"

"I have not seen it," Thi Xin said. But Madame Phuong told me what had happened. The poor little thing will have to go to the orphanage as soon as it is old enough to leave us, because nobody knows who the mother was, or whether she had a husband."

Mary nodded and looked down at the table.

"The mother is in the mortuary, she was so young to die, and if no one comes to claim her body she will get nothing but a cheap pauper's funeral. It's terrible to think that she'll just be quickly buried out of the way, with no one to shed a single tear over her grave."

It was not a cheerful subject and they relapsed into silence again. It was early, but this had been an exhausting day and they had nothing left to do, and so they prepared for bed. Thi Xin said, "good night," quietly, and then turned her face to her pillow and tried to sleep, while Mary remained awake for a while longer and tried to read. However, tonight the English landscape of meadows, groves and streams, conjured up by the lines of Wordsworth failed to calm her thoughts. She reached the lines, *The rainbow comes and goes, And lovely is the rose,* and stopped with a feeling of bitterness. Where, she wondered, were the rainbows and roses for Vietnam? Surely these people were entitled to their share of sunshine and birdsong, but when and where?

******

The two nurses were awakened abruptly the next morning by the thunder of aircraft sweeping low overhead, and they both sat upright with a sharp attack of fright. The reverberations faded as they looked anxiously across the room at each other, and then Mary swung her legs out of her bed and began to pull a dressing gown on top of her nightdress.

"Where are you going?" Thi Xin asked.

"To the roof," Mary answered. "To see what's happening."

The Vietnamese girl hesitated, and then she too got out of bed and found her dressing gown. Together they went outside to the landing, and then hurried up the narrow stairs that led to the flat roof. The sun was very bright and dazzling, and in the blue but in places smoke-stained sky above the more distant area of Cholon they saw more planes wheeling and circling like fat angry moths trying to approach a hostile candle flame. The planes were the dumpy little Skyraiders, but far to the left two fish-bowl helicopter gunships were also heading for the scene. Streaks of white smoke lanced down from the wings of one of the Skyraiders.

"They are firing rockets at the Viet Cong positions," Thi Xin said in a small, frightened voice.

"The fools!" Mary said in exasperation. "When will the Americans realize that bombs and rockets do more harm than good. They'll kill more civilians and destroy more property than anything else."

"Those are not American planes." Thi Xin had very sharp eyes. "They are Marshal Ky's Vietnamese Air Force. But it does not really matter because the ordinary people usually believe that anything which flies is American. The Americans will have to take the blame. "

"It's stupid, whoever is responsible! It's insane!" Mary felt as though she wanted to stamp her foot or cry, because already she

144

could visualize the increased flow of torn and mutilated patients pouring into the hospital wards.

Thi Xin watched for another moment and then said nervously:

"Perhaps we should go below."

Mary nodded and they returned to the apartment to wash and dress, and then to make their beds and tidy up, and finally to prepare some breakfast. While they were finishing their coffee the telephone rang on the landing outside their door, and after a moment's hesitation Mary set down her cup and went to answer it. She picked up the receiver and gave their own number, and then recognized the anxious voice of Doctor Phuong.

"Hello, Nurse Francis? I am so glad that I have caught you in time. It will not be safe for either you or Thi Xin to come into the hospital today, and so I must tell you both to stay in your apartment until you hear from me again. Perhaps it will be best if you keep the outer doors locked and do not go outside at all. Even if you have no food it will not harm you to go hungry for a couple of days."

"But why, what is wrong?"

Doctor Phuong sounded astonished.

"Can't you hear the airplanes?"

"Yes — but they are several miles away."

"They are bombing Cholon and they are still too close for safety. The Government has started its counter-offensive and things are much worse than they were last night. Large units of Government troops are trying to clear the streets and there is much fighting. You must stay where you are."

"We should not have come home last night," Mary said, feeling guilty. "If we have to be stranded then it is better to be stranded at the hospital where we can be useful, even if we have to sleep on the floor."

"It is too late to think of that now."

"We can try to get through."

"No," Phuong objected sharply. "I will not permit that. The streets are too dangerous."

"We can try," Mary insisted. "If we run into trouble we can always turn back, and if we get through we can stay at the hospital until things calm down. You will be very busy. We shall be needed there."

"1 forbid it," Phuong said in agitation. "There is too much risk. I order you to stay at home."

Mary had been in Asia long enough to understand the value of bland politeness, and she said carefully;

"I am sorry, Doctor Phuong, I cannot hear you. There is some interference on the line."

"But it is a perfect line. I can hear no interference — and I expressly — "

"Hello, Doctor Phuong? Doctor Phuong are you there, I can't hear — "

Mary deliberately interrupted him, and then just as deliberately hung up in the middle of her own sentence. She hesitated for a moment, and then to make sure that he did not call her back to renew the argument she lifted the receiver and laid it on the table beside the phone. She turned to find Thi Xin watching her.

"You don't have to come," she explained. "Doctor Phuong has forbidden it. I was only speaking for myself."

"Doctor Ton Thu will be there," Thi Xin said. She was being honest but after a moment she added seriously; "But even if he was not I think that I would still come with you."

Mary smiled, and then they both fastened their capes around their shoulders and went down to their bicycles. Mary was still confident that their uniforms would protect them from any deliberate harm by either side, but she found that her heart was beating more noticeably than usual as she wheeled her bicycle out into the deserted street. Thi Xin's pale bronze face showed signs of nervousness, as though her weaker spirit had already begun to falter. They mounted their machines and began to pedal swiftly towards the hospital.

On the first part of their route the streets were quiet and deserted, although above their heads the Skyraiders still buzzed, and all around them they could hear the spiteful crackle of distant gun battles. Loud but muffled explosions reached their ears and as they sped hurriedly along it became obvious that they were heading directly into the more hotly contested areas. Fear caused them to pedal furiously and they could only pray that they would reach their goal without being hit. They passed several abandoned cars, some of them over-turned and burned-out, and it seemed that the city had sickened into an ugly rash of shell pockmarks and broken windows. On the pavements the black flotsam of the refugees moved aimlessly or huddled into doorways, while those fortunate inhabitants who had homes stayed behind their barred doors. No shops were open, although a few showed signs of looting.

They came to a road junction and heard a heavy, clanking rumble, and then violent sounds of gunfire frighteningly close on their left. Mary glanced swiftly sideways and both girls hunched low on their cycles as they flashed past. A squad of Government soldiers was advancing down the street behind a tank, and obviously there were Viet Cong defending some of the houses. The scene was gone as swiftly as it appeared but the sound of weapons exploding seemed to follow them. Their legs were already aching and trembling, but together they tried to force a little more speed out of their racing bicycles.

They had almost reached the hospital, and it seemed that they had run the gauntlet of the shells and bullets that flew blindly through the now shrieking streets, and then they had to cross their last major road junction. As they did so a machine gun began spitting streams of bullets from their right and the plate-glass fronts of the corner shops shattered into a million flying pieces on their left. The machine gun had been set up behind a barricade of oil drums which the Viet Cong guerrillas had built across the mouth of the street, and it missed them by a matter of seconds in time. Further up the opposite street mouth another squad of ARVIN soldiers were trying to get to grips as they advanced from doorway to doorway, and both sides momentarily held their fire, more out of startled bewilderment than conscience as the two nurses with their distinctive capes flying darted between them. Only one guerrilla with a recoilless rifle failed to see them appear and pulled the trigger. The shell was thrown on to the opposite pavement just behind the two speeding bicycles, and the explosion tore up the curbstone and threw a large slab of concrete into the spokes of Thi Xin's back wheel. The Vietnamese girl screamed as her cycle was hurled sideways, and then she smashed into Mary and they both went down in a skidding tangle of limbs and machines.

For a moment they were helpless, but fortunately the skid and their own momentum carried them out of the direct line of fire and deposited them in a confused heap in the gutter on the opposite side of the crossroads. Mary found herself an undignified part of a heap of rotting refuse with both bicycles piled on top of her, and only by throwing up her arms did she protect her face and head from a knockout blow on the edge of the pavement. Instead she bruised and grazed her elbows and badly lacerated her right knee. Thi Xin had somehow sailed over her head and rolled along the road, and she picked herself up and began to run like a terrified doe, proving that at least her legs were unbroken. Mary crawled out more slowly from beneath the two bicycles, and although she was dazed and hurt it registered in her mind that her own machine appeared relatively undamaged by the crash. She dragged it free and then began to run painfully after Thi Xin. A chorus of angry shouts and curses followed them, but no more bullets.

When Mary caught up with her friend she was limping badly, and she found that Thi Xin had ripped her sleeve and cut her arm, and had collected a purpling bruise and a cut above her right eye. They were both covered in dust and dirt and wincing from their pains, but at least they had suffered no major injury. Mary seated herself astride her bicycle again and then said grimly:

"We're nearly there. Get on the crossbar."

Thi Xin looked at her hesitantly, but Mary was determined and the sound of the battle was still close. Reluctantly the Vietnamese girl positioned herself on the hard iron bar of the bicycle, and held on to Mary's shoulder with one hand. Mary pushed the machine into movement with her feet, and then found the pedals and wobbled precariously for a minute before she worked up to speed and maintained her balance. Thi Xin un-heroically closed her eyes and they began the last lap of their frantic race to the hospital.

Mary's right knee was hurting her intensely but she strove to ignore it and concentrated all her energy into turning the pedals even faster. For the next few minutes they progressed almost as furiously as before, and she began to be thankful that she had selected a man's cycle that would carry them both. The strain on her heart and lungs was beginning to throw a blurred veil across her eyes, and then suddenly a Skyraider thundered low over their heads and startled her. She swerved, and then too late saw an unexpected crater in the road ahead where a mortar shell had ripped up the surface. She wrenched on the brakes and the bicycle skidded, and then they both tumbled over the handlebars again as the front wheel lurched into the hole.

The two girls were badly shaken again, but although they picked themselves up more slowly they could find no additional damage to themselves other than an extra coating of dirt. However, the front wheel of the cycle was hopelessly buckled. Mary hauled the machine out of the crater, glared at it, and then threw it angrily to the side of the road.

"Sod it," she said, because it seemed an appropriate time to use the worst swear word in her vocabulary. "We shall have to walk."

Thi Xin looked relieved and they continued on foot. Mary was limping but the crack of rifle bullets from somewhere nearby made them break into a run, and without looking back to find out whether they were in any real danger or not they sprinted the last few hundred yards to the hospital. They arrived at the front entrance disheveled and straining for breath, and stumbled weakly up the steps into the small reception hall. Madame Phuong saw them from behind the desk and raised a sharp cry of alarm, and then her husband came running.

Doctor Phuong stopped when he saw them and held up his hands in horror. Then he clasped his hands together fiercely and his face became stern and angry.

"You are two foolish young ladies," he told them passionately. "I told you to stay away! I warned you that the streets were unsafe and that the Government troops were fighting with the Viet Cong. You could have been killed!"

Neither of his two nurses had the breath to answer and he looked them over and unclasped his hands to make another expansive gesture of despair.

"Look at yourselves! Your clothes are torn! You are both covered with dirt! You have hurt yourselves! What has happened to you?"

"We fell off our bicycles," Mary managed at last.

"But I told you not to come! I expressly forbade you to come! And you, Mademoiselle! You hung up the telephone while I was talking!"

Mary could not deny it, and the Vietnamese Doctor glared at her and became silent. Phuong shook his head sadly and swallowed hard, and then he was choked with a new emotion. He stepped forwards and rested his hands on their shoulders and said in a broken voice:

"You are two very foolish young ladies, but I thank you for it. You should have obeyed me, but I thank you for coming.

CHAPTER NINE

On that second day of the Communist Tet Offensive the big battle for Vietnam raged throughout the length and breadth of the agony-stricken country. In one ferocious onslaught the Viet Cong had carried the war out of the jungles and into the cities and towns and airfields, but then the essence of surprise was lost and the counter-offensive became a bloody slugging match between the two sides, with the civilian population as always trapped in the middle. In the capital bitter street fighting ebbed and flowed in the suburbs, and in Gia Dinh and Cholon countless fires burned. The Skyraider pilots blitzed their own city with air strikes, and around Tan Son Nhut American helicopters used their merciless fire-power in an orgy of self defense.

At his breakfast table Vu Phan Quang sat tense and tight-lipped, listening to the nightmare sounds which flared all around the villa. He had spent a practically sleepless night and he was a badly worried man. Opposite him sat Mai Ahn, her face pale but still lovely and composed, although this morning she had drawn her two sons closer on either side. The two boys were both solemn and quiet; Vu Truong Quang was now thirteen years old, and his younger brother Vu Truong Phan was seven. Both boys were wearing white shirts with red and grey striped neckties and dark short trousers, their school uniform, although it was obvious that there would be no school for them today. Quang also wore a white shirt, with a dark red tie and the brown trousers of his suit. Only Mai Ahn still favored the Vietnamese clothes which gave an added grace to her oriental beauty. She wore a high collared blue tunic, split up to both hips over white silk trousers.

The table was spread with a spotless white cloth, and the tableware was of expensive silver. There were two racks of lightly browned toast, two dishes of butter, and a selection of jam preserves and honey, but none of them were eating with more than half an appetite. Quang had spread his first slice of toast with butter and then sugar, a family favorite, but he had yet to eat. Mai Ahn lifted the silver coffee pot from its stand and looked at him enquiringly, and he nodded. She poured him his third cup of coffee, and said quietly:

"If it becomes necessary I think the soldiers can protect us. The Lieutenant seems to be a very polite and capable young man."

She was referring to the ARVIN squad that had been detailed to defend the villa, for Quang was now a very influential man, and as a Government minister his home was an obvious target for attack. Quang pursed his lips and was about to tell her that a squad was insufficient, however polite their Lieutenant, but before he could speak a mortar coughed and a shell exploded in the villa garden.

The younger boy screamed as the fountain of dirt and shrubs and flower blossoms blew up in front of the window, and as Mai Ahn jerked back in alarm hot coffee splashed out from the jug in her hand and spilled over the table. The white cloth was ruined and Truong Quang howled as the hot liquid scalded the back of his wrist. Two chairs crashed over as he sprang upright in the same moment as his father. Mai Ahn had automatically grabbed the younger boy into her arms, dropping the coffee pot on to the floor in the same moment, and then Quang rushed round the table to grab at them both.

"Quickly!" he shouted. "Get into the bedroom."

Their old servant had come running and was almost trampled as Quang herded his family frantically through the door. In the gardens outside they could hear the soldiers who had been bivouacked in tents shouting and running, and then a second mortar shell was lobbed accurately through the dining room window. Quang threw himself forward as the glass smashed and his weight carried them all out into the hall, and as they tumbled down the mortar shell landed between the toast racks and shattered the breakfast table which they had only just left behind.

"My home! My children!"

Mai Ahn cried out almost hysterically as the dishes of honey and butter and fragments of shell casing sprayed through the doorway to spatter or gouge into the opposite wall, and the younger boy also burst into a flood of terrified tears and wailing. Quang was sprawling half on top of them and he cursed as he picked himself up. He glanced back once into the wrecked shambles of the dining room and then said angrily:

"Be quiet. All of you into the bedroom."

He lifted his wife and his sobbing seven-year-old to their feet and urged them ahead of him again. His eldest son had fallen down in a tangle with the old servant and it was difficult to tell who was helping who as they scrambled up together and hurried in his wake. Quang rushed them all up the stairs and then thrust open the door of the main bedroom and bundled them all inside. He ran over to the window and gazed down for a second into the villa grounds. The soldiers who had been detailed to protect his property were still running to and fro in apparent confusion below the palm fronds, and he saw one man stretched dead in a flower bed. Automatic rifles cracked back and forth and another mortar shell blasted a section of the outer wall into flying rubble. Quang was dry-mouthed and his heart was pounding as though the blood in his veins was pouring through it like a river in violent flood. He swallowed hard, and then bit his lip as he leaned out of the window and quickly pulled in the shutters. They were specially reinforced shutters of light steel which he had installed long ago for an eventuality such as this, and he breathed more easily when they were closed and barred.

He turned to find Mai Ahn with her back to the far wall, staring at him with horrified eyes, and with her two sons clasped close. The servant, a frail old man whom they had inherited with the villa from the old mandarin who had died in one of Diem's prison camps so many years ago, stood by helplessly. All of them were waiting for Quang to decide what had to be done, and so Quang had to fight down his own terror. His cardinal rule was simply to survive, preferably in luxury, and preferably by scheming rather than by open fighting, but this was one time when he could not run. And this time he had his wife and his sons to consider.

"All of you sit down," he ordered, "with your backs to the wall."

Mai Ahn hesitated, but then she lowered herself to a sitting position and pulled the two boys down beside her. Quang turned away from them and hurled the sheets and pillows from the double bed, and then he dragged the heavy foam mattress towards them. The old man moved forward in a faltering effort to help, but he was too slow to serve any useful purpose in this emergency.

"You too," snapped Quang. "Sit down."

The old man obeyed, and Quang positioned the mattress so that it leaned against the wall, covering them from any fall of plaster or flying shell splinters that might occur. Mai Ahn reached out her hand to pull him down with them, but Quang shook her hand away. The mattress would not protect them if the Viet Cong broke in, and he knew that he could expect no mercy for any of them. The Communist guerrillas were behaving more or less correctly towards ordinary civilians, but at the same time they were ruthlessly murdering the families of Government employees or serving soldiers.

"Stay there," Quang commanded. "And do not move."

He ran to the dressing table and pulled open a drawer. Inside was a 0.45 Colt revolver and he broke the barrel and swiftly began to thrust shells into the empty chambers. His hands were sweating and his thumb slipped several times as he pressed the shells into place, and then he snapped the loaded revolver shut. He turned and saw that Truong Quang had disobeyed him and emerged tentatively from behind the barrier he had made.

"Father," The boy was white-faced but his voice was steady, and there was a flushed red stain over the back of his right wrist where he had been scalded by the hot coffee. "Is there another gun?"

Quang bit his lip and shook his head, and for a fleeting moment he wondered where his son had acquired his courage. Perhaps it was a strain descended from his grandfather.

"No," he said. "But your place is to stay with your mother and your brother."

The boy nodded, and then turned and knelt to crawl back behind the mattress. Quang left them and hurried back on to the landing at the top of the stairs.

The front doors were smashed inwards in the same moment and he dropped to one knee behind the banister post with the revolver leveled ready to fire. A handful of men burst into the small hallway, but they had their backs to him and were firing outwards, and he recognized the polite Lieutenant and the uniforms of his South Vietnamese soldiers. It seemed as though the grounds had already been lost to the Viet Cong, and Quang ran back into the main bedroom to the telephone. He had to lay down the revolver for a moment as he picked up the phone, and he dialed a number with a shaking finger that could barely find the figures.

It took him three minutes to get an answer, which in the circumstances was a fast reply; but it was three minutes of sweating and biting his lip, and listening to his stately home being reduced to a smoking shell and rubble around him. One blast brought half the plaster down from the ceiling, and another severely buckled the steel shutters across the window. Quang crouched and hunched his shoulders in the middle of the floor, and then he was through.

"General," he shouted frantically. "This is Vu Phan Quang. My home is being attacked. You must send me some more soldiers! A company at least, or a battalion!"

His old friend uttered a sardonic laugh.

"Monsieur Quang, there are no companies, or battalions in reserve. As fast as our troop units are re-called to the city we are throwing them out into the streets to fight the Viet Cong."

"But the Viet Cong are here! Thousands of them! At any minute they will break into my house!"

"The Viet Cong are everywhere," the General retorted un-sympathetically. "They are in every street, every house, and every courtyard. I am sorry but you are wasting my time."

"General!" Quang all but howled. "We shall be killed! You and I are old friends, you must — "

He stopped as he realized that the line had gone dead. There had been no click to indicate that the General had hung up, and he knew that somewhere the line had been neatly cut. He cursed and then exchanged the receiver for his revolver and ran back to the landing.

He arrived just as a superbly pitched mortar shell came through the shattered front door and exploded in the hall, killing the polite young Lieutenant and most of the surviving soldiers who had rallied around him.

Quang was frozen with horror, and he realized that he had not even known the young Lieutenant's name. Now the officer was just one of a litter of broken and blood-streaked bodies that had been thrown around the smoking ruins of the hallway. For a moment there was a dark silence, and then shouts of triumph echoed from the garden and Quang became aware that the enemy guerrillas were rushing forward to seal their victory with a forced entry into the villa itself. One of the sprawled soldiers stirred and groaned, but there was no one left who was capable of stopping the invasion and fear gave movement to Quang's paralyzed limbs as he ran in great leaps down the stairs. He fired his revolver twice through the doorway and saw startled men reel back to either side. Then he dropped the revolver and scooped up the submachine gun that had fallen with the young Lieutenant. Bullets smashed into the already splintered paneling of the staircase, but then he let rip an answering burst with the submachine gun and heard a scream from outside.

The attack was briefly repelled, but the clamor of voices told him that the odds were too hot, and also he was afraid that the mortar gunner might lob another shell through the doorway now that he had found the range so precisely. A retreat was the only sane course, but Quang paused to pick up his revolver and thrust it into his waistband. He glanced once at the groaning soldier who showed signs of life, but then a bullet snapped through the doorway and smashed the hanging pieces of glass which were all that was left of the large hall mirror into even smaller splinters. One sliver stung Quang sharply and deeply in the side of the neck, and without another thought for the dying man beside him he bounded hastily back up the stairs.

He reached the landing and then turned on one knee, crouching with the submachine gun at the ready. He could feel the warm blood trickling down his neck and seeping into the white collar of his shirt but he ignored it. He waited for the Viet Cong regulars who charged into the hallway below behind a shield of blazing automatic weapons, and then he fired down on their heads and added their reckless forms to the pile of bodies that were mounting up in the doorway.

He backed up to the bedroom and felt that now he could only sell his life dearly. The need to protect his wife and sons gave him courage that he had never before possessed and he vowed silently that he would defend them while he lived. There was no escape, and there was nothing else that he could do. He looked back and saw the white faces of Mai Ahn and Truong Phan peeping out from beneath the mattress against the wall, and there was grief in his heart that rose up to choke him. Mai Ahn saw the blood on the collar and the shoulder of his white shirt and began to scramble towards him.

"Phan Quang, you are hurt."

"A scratch," he insisted. "Stay back."

She ran to him despite his command and caught at his arm. He shook his head irritably as she tried to examine the slight but messy wound and then retreated into the bedroom to push her out of the line of fire. Roughly he shook her away and thrust her down into the shelter, and in the same moment another shell landing on the roof collapsed the bedroom next door and brought more plaster raining down from the ceiling.

"Stay down," Quang said desperately. And then he saw that his eldest son was again standing upright and clear of the mattress which he had arranged for their protection.

Quang hesitated, but he knew that it would soon be over. He took the revolver from his waist and held it out to the boy. Truong Quang bit his lip and then took the offered weapon.

"If I am killed, then you must defend your mother," Quang said grimly.

Then he turned and went back to the doorway to kneel and cover the landing with his submachine gun.

His son stood behind him in the centre of the bedroom with the revolver.

Quang waited.

CHAPTER TEN

The Viet Cong section surrounding the half demolished ruins of the villa were delayed by a short battle to mop up the remnants of the ARVIN squad that had been bivouacked in the gardens. A Sergeant with a group of young soldiers had been pinned down in a corner behind the pitifully slender trunks of some palm trees, and their line of fire covered the villa entrance where their Lieutenant had been killed. The fire-fight was short and sharp, and was simply resolved by two of the guerrillas who wriggled backwards out of the gardens and then ran around the outer road to toss two grenades over the six-foot walls. The last pocket of resistance was shattered and the leading guerrillas were free to rush the doorway. Their section leader had witnessed the fall of his comrades in the previous assault, and as they crashed into the villa with all guns blazing he automatically wheeled and swung his combat rifle upwards to spray bullets up the staircase. In the same moment the two men who had been left in the street died, cut down by a platoon of advancing Government soldiers. The Captain in charge of the newly arrived ARVIN platoon had orders to clear this suburb, and having fallen on a pocket of Viet Cong from behind he lost no time in pressing his advantage. He shouted an order and his soldiers surged into the attack.

******

On the upper floor of the villa Quang shot down the Viet Cong section leader and the first of his men as they attempted to storm the staircase and burst over the top of the landing. The bodies fell back to scatter the living men below but in the same moment the submachine gun in Quang's hands ceased its vibrating stutter, even though his finger was still tight on the trigger. He realized that the magazine was empty and his face broke into the misery of tears. In the next rush they would kill him, and then his son, and then — it was more than he could bear to think of and he lowered the empty submachine gun to the floor and pressed his face into his hands.

From below he heard the sounds of renewed conflict, more screams and shouting voices, and the increased clamor of weapons singing their hymns of death and hate.

Truong Quang had moved uncertainly to the window, and it was he who peeped through a gap in the buckled plates of the steel shutter and then cried hoarsely:

"Father, there are more soldiers in the garden — our soldiers, they wear our uniforms!"

Quang lifted his head and straightened his shoulders. He stared out on to the landing through the reeking fumes of faint blue cordite smoke, and for a moment he could not believe that there was to be no second attempt to storm the staircase. Then he scrambled to his feet and ran back to his son. Through the shutter he too saw the ARVIN soldiers swarming across the torn and trampled flower beds below, and he threw his arm around the boy's slender shoulders and crushed him tightly.

"We are saved," he almost sobbed, and then louder so that Mai Ahn could hear him above the noise. "More soldiers have arrived. We are saved!"

He turned away from the window and then looked down at his son. Truong Quang gazed up into his face and he was still scared, his own tooth-marks showed sharply on his lower lip and he was trembling. The heavy Colt revolver shook slightly in his small hand, which still showed the angry red flush where he had been scalded. Father and son regarded each other for a moment and then Quang gently retrieved the revolver. He did not want his son to see the tears of relief that were forming in his own eyes, and so he said huskily:

"Go back to your mother now. I will stand by the door until it is finished."

******

Ten minutes passed before they could safely descend, and by then the Viet Cong assault force had been shot dead to the last man. The

ARVIN were taking no prisoners and showing no mercy. Their Captain, who had the name tape Thinh sewn across his breast, had a wife and children of his own, and he knew that the Viet Cong were not hesitating to slaughter the wives and children of his brother officers.

Quang had donned his jacket to cover some of the bloodstains on his shirt and tried to attain a little formal dignity as he thanked the Captain for saving all their lives. Then he looked around the debris that remained of his home and added somewhat bitterly:

"It is a pity that you could not have arrived sooner. Now there is very little left for you to protect."

Captain Thinh shrugged his shoulders and said politely:

"I am afraid that in any case we cannot stay here to protect you. My task is to clear this suburb. We must move on to seek out more Viet Cong."

Quang stared at him and said in agitation:

"But after you have gone the Viet Cong may make another attack here. I am a Government minister. Surely your first task is to protect my home!"

"Those were not my orders," Thinh said apologetically. "I am sorry, Monsieur Quang."

Quang would have argued, but then he looked round slowly and accepted that his home was now nothing more than a death-tainted heap of ruins and rubble that was not worth defending.

"It does not matter," he said resignedly. "I have an apartment in the city, and I will take my family there. You must do your duty."

Thinh nodded, and with the issue settled he returned to his men and they prepared to depart.

Mai Ahn looked distraught and heartbroken as she gazed around what was left of the villa, but there was no time to comfort her now. Quang told her to pack what things she would need and sent the old servant to help her, and then he went to rescue his car from the garage beside the house. The doors and one corner of the wall had been blown down, and inside the large Japanese Toyota saloon that had been his pride and joy had suffered a large amount of superficial damage. The windshield was smashed and the gleaming black paintwork scratched and covered in brick dust, while the offside wing had been badly buckled and crushed. With his bare hands Quang wrenched and pulled at the wing until he had cleared it from the wheel, and then he brushed the worst of the broken glass off the front seats and climbed inside. The car started when he turned the ignition key and he drove it out on to the driveway, lurching over part of the fallen wall.

He went back to help Mai Ahn and collect his sons, hurrying because Thinh and his soldiers were already moving away. Mai Ahn had packed a suitcase with spare clothes and the old servant was carrying it slowly down the stairs. Quang grabbed it from him and urged them all out to the car. The suitcase he threw into the boot and then he hustled Mai Ahn and his sons into the back seat.

The old servant held back."I will stay," the old man said, "to defend our home from bad people and looters."

Quang hesitated, and then decided that the old man was part of the family.

"The only looters will be Viet Cong, and they will kill you."

"It is my duty."

"Get in the car," Quang snapped, and pulled him inside.

With no more arguments he slipped in the clutch and drove out into the main road, swinging right and heading fast into the centre of Saigon.

******

They reached the apartment after twenty minutes of erratic driving and several bad frights, but without encountering any solid obstacles. Once clear of the suburbs they had escaped the worst of the fighting, and the centre of the city was an oasis of rigid suspense, baking under the hot sun and cringing under the palls of smoke and the screaming overhead passes of the Skyraiders. Mai Ahn had been at a loss to understand where they were going, but when the car drew to a halt she immediately recognized what had been their old home during the early days of their marriage. After their move to the villa Quang had told her that he had sold it, and now she looked at him with uncertain eyes. Quang's mind was busy with getting them all off the dangerous streets and under cover, and he failed to notice that anything was wrong.

Like a shepherd with a bewildered flock he herded them all ahead of him, pausing only to grab up the suitcase from the boot before he brought up the rear. They ascended the stairs and then there was a delay while he found his key to let them in. They clustered in the small outer room with its adjoining kitchen and Quang dumped the case and turned to close the door.

"If we are safe anywhere, then we shall be safe here," he told them. "But we will stay inside this house and remain quiet and show no lights until the fighting is over. We do not want to attract any attention."

The two boys and the old servant nodded, and Quang was too preoccupied to notice that Mai Ahn was exhibiting more curiosity to their surroundings than attention to his words.

"I think I will remove the electricity fuses," Quang said. "Then no one will make a mistake and show a light."

"Father," Truong Quang had been patient and brave, but he could be so no longer. "My hand is burning."

Quang remembered his son's scalded wrist.

"There is some butter," he said doubtfully. "Perhaps that will soothe it. Come with me into the kitchen."

Mai Ahn watched them go, and then left her younger son and the old servant standing uncertainly in the centre of the room. She entered the bedroom and closed the door behind her. There were many things to remember about this room, but it was not a moment for memories. The lilac blue drapes were drawn across the window, but enough light filtered through to show up all the details. She looked at the large double bed, neatly made up, and then at its reflection in the ceiling mirror that had not been there before. As she moved forward her own image came into view, gazing down at her with dark, almond eyes that were numbed and bruised with inner pain. The white carpet was soft under her feet, and more expensive than the one that had been there before, and she looked slowly around the erotic paintings with their tangled limbs and bare flesh that adorned the walls. She noted the bowl of fresh fruit and the brandy bottle and glasses upon the bedside table, and tentatively she ran her fingers over the backs of the collection of books. She could not read their titles, but she drew one from its place and looked without expression at the line drawing on its cover. Everything had been changed and her suspicions were confirmed. She had suspected for a long time and now she knew.

She heard the door open behind her and turned slowly.

Quang stood there, and his smooth face showed more shock and anguish. In the excitement he had forgotten this room until he had looked up from tending his son's hand and noticed her absence, and now he knew that he had committed a colossal blunder, although in the circumstances there was nowhere else that he could have taken them. He closed the door again but did not know what to say. He could only flinch from her hurt, accusing eyes.

"The Frenchwoman," Mai Ahn said quietly, and it was a statement and not a question.

Quang nodded and bit his lip, and then said desperately:

"But it is finished. It is over now!" The plea was true because he had decided that Suzanne's husband was too dangerous and too difficult to kill. He went on earnestly: "After this morning it is over — after what *we* have just been through!"

Mai Ann said nothing, and after a moment he ran across the room and began to tear down the lurid pictures from the walls. He did not want his sons to see those. He thrust them into

174

a drawer in the bedside table and then stared up in agitation at the long mirror above the bed. Without a screwdriver he couldn't get it down and his own face taunted him.

Mai Ahn watched and still said nothing. While the servant and her children were within hearing she would not make a scene.

******

In Cholon the Viet Cong had occupied the streets surrounding the hospital, and now they controlled almost the whole of the old Chinese city. This was their stronghold and the ARVIN was making only half-hearted efforts to get them out. A civil war was a distasteful and bloody affair and the Viet Cong were not afraid to die.

In the hospital itself the routine work went on as always, except that the influx of maimed and dead and dying had reached monstrous proportions. There was little that could be done for them under such pressure except to separate those who might live from those who would not, and Phuong and Keller worked non-stop in the operating theatre on a table that dripped with blood beneath the stark white disc of the overhead light. The two intern doctors were also working at full pitch, and today they were turning away the usual queues of sad-eyed and suffering people with their coughs and sores and sicknesses, and admitting only the war-wounded.

There was no respite for the nurses either, which was perhaps a blessing in disguise for it gave them no time to worry over what might be happening outside the hospital. Mary had fed Phat Sang's tiny, premature baby, which had been the only bright spot in her morning. The infant needed time to suck the warm milk from the bottle which she held carefully to its mouth, and it was one job which could not be hurried. Afterwards she replaced the baby in its cot, and smiled as the little girl closed her pin-slit eyes in sleepy satisfaction. Mary returned to help Thi Xin in the squalor of the children's ward and limped stiffly as she hurried along. Her knee was still smarting because she and Thi Xin had painted each other's wounds with iodine.

They tended only the children who were more seriously ill, and had to entrust the others to the ministrations of their mothers and grandmothers who squatted beside their beds. Today they had little time to supervise and they had to decide which were the priority cases. More mangled little bodies were admitted and had to be found space on the floor, and then there were the orphans who had no relatives to care for them who had to be looked after. The orphans were kept together at one end of the ward, where they watched the doors with slack eyes, waiting for parents who never came, and who were most probably dead. Most of them had been brought in from the countryside after American attacks or patrols.

One of the smaller boys had to be changed, and while Mary fitted him into a clean pair of pajama trousers Thi Xin wiped clean the plastic bed sheet on which he had lain with two heavily bandaged companions. Mary held the child while Thi Xin finished her task, holding him carefully because of the severe napalm burns that had taken most of the skin from his white-swathed arm, and then suddenly the doors behind them burst open. Mary turned sharply with the boy still in her arms, and saw a group of five ragged little Vietnamese in dark plaid shirts and black cotton trousers burst into the ward. The men all had tense, tight-lipped faces and gripped combat rifles in their hands, leveled and ready to fire.

"Viet Cong!"

Thi Xin had also turned and cried out in horror, and then the leader of the five men shouted at her to be silent. He was a short young man with long, sleek black hair, and his whole body seemed to quiver as though his limbs were molded around coiled springs instead of normal bones. He stared at Mary, noting her blue eyes and white skin and her dark gold hair, but then Thi Xin rushed between them.

"This is a hospital," she said fiercely. "There is no war here. Please go away and leave us alone!"

The young Viet Cong barely looked at her. He lifted his combat rifle and pressed the barrel against her shoulder to move her aside, leaving a long oil mark across her starched white dress. The combat rifle pointed at Mary, and the guerrilla had only one word.

"American?"

"No!" Thi Xin said sharply, again in Vietnamese. "She is English. She is a nurse. This is a hospital for children. There is no war here. Your war is outside."

"Our war is everywhere," the youth said coldly. "Only when Vietnam is liberated will there be no war." His slit eyes gazed steadily at Mary and he accused again: "American."

The little boy in Mary's arms began to cry. She looked down at the distorted face and then realized that she was holding him across her breast almost as a shield. Hurriedly she turned and laid the child in his cot out of harm's way, and then she faced the armed Vietnamese again. She was afraid and she felt sure that she was going to be killed, for she could see nothing but fanaticism in the young man's gaze. The light of glory was in his eyes, and to kill or be killed meant nothing because he was part of a supreme cause that was far above the value of any single human life. He would kill or die for

Communism just as other men had killed and died for Christ or Mohammed, or a score of other Gods and religions, or as the Americans would kill or die for Peace and the American Dream. Nothing would come before his cause.

Mary's mouth was dry and her heart was running wild, but she swallowed hard and made what seemed a pointless denial.

"No, I'm English."

"English," Thi Xin repeated in Vietnamese. And then she closed her hand over the muzzle of the combat rifle and pushed it away. *"She is English!"* she almost shrieked for the third time. "That is not the same as American. She is a nurse. She is here only to help our sick children. Look around you! There is nothing here that can make any difference to your war. What can you gain by killing nurses and children in a hospital?"

The young Viet Cong scowled into her appealing face and his own expression revealed nothing of his thoughts. He was silent and he knew that he could blow off the restraining hand and kill the white girl all with the same bullet if he cared to pull the trigger of his rifle. However, he sensed that his comrades had grown uncomfortable behind him, and there was a hair-line of difference between a patriot and a murderer. The Vietnamese nurse was right and there was no action here that could further his cause, and slowly he began to relax.

The light went out of his eyes and he drew back his combat rifle, and then in that precise moment of agonized silence Richard Keller walked unsuspecting into the far end of the ward.

CHAPTER ELEVEN

Keller was weary for he had just completed his fourth successive operation of that morning. All of them had been rushed emergencies and he had been forced to throw out his prepared schedule for the day. However, there was one nine-year old girl in the children's ward with a shell-shattered foot which had turned gangrenous, and which he had intended to amputate above the ankle, and he had come to check on her condition. If the foot was no worse he could postpone the operation for another day, but if the gangrene showed signs of spreading higher then he would tell the nurses to prepare the child for the theatre. He walked with his head slightly bowed and in his concentrated mind there was no room for any thought which was not connected with the work that had to be done, and as he entered the doorway he did not even notice the group of armed Viet Cong at the far end of the ward.

The five combat rifles flashed back into a threatening position and for the moment Mary was forgotten. The tall surgeon with his confident though preoccupied manner was their new target, and the black-haired youth shouted his single word of condemnation like a challenging curse.

"American!"

Keller lifted his head and then stopped dead. His grey eyes were startled, but then they became calm and he merely pressed his lips more tightly together. He had given no conscious speculation to what might happen if the Viet Cong invaded the hospital, and yet it was not entirely unexpected. He was careful to keep his hands innocently at his sides and began to walk slowly down the narrow aisle between the crowded beds. The frightened eyes of the child patients and their squatting relatives watched.

Thi Xin moved again, shifting her slim body like a delicate reed attempting to shield an advancing oak. She kept her hand pressed over the leveled muzzle of the foremost combat rifle and said with new desperation:

"No. He is not American. He is also English. He is an English doctor who has come to help us."

"You tell me lies, little sister."

The young guerrilla was angry and he leaned forward and grabbed at her wrist. He twisted sharply and Thi Xin's hand was wrenched away from the barrel of his rifle. He twisted her arm further to force her out of the way, but then Keller had reached them and he stopped. They stared at each other for a moment, and then Keller moved his hands slowly and placed them on Thi Xin's shoulders.

"It's alright, nurse," he said quietly.

Thi Xin looked up into the steady grey eyes. The young Vietnamese released her wrist in order to bring his finger back to the trigger of his rifle, and then Keller moved the nurse aside in a more gentle manner.

The five rifles pointed at Keller and Mary could only watch helplessly. It was impossible to try and reason with the five Viet Cong because she could not speak enough of their language, and against five rifles she could do nothing physical. She could only wait, knowing that if they killed Keller then next they would kill her, and that any resistance would only mean that an unnecessary number of their helpless patients would also be killed in the shooting.

The leading guerrilla spoke again with bitter conviction.

"American."

Keller could grasp enough Vietnamese to understand what Thi Xin had tried to say on his behalf. He could support that lie, but he had no desire to hide himself behind a false label. He was not ashamed of his nationality, and nor of the more war-like presence of the great mass of his countrymen here in Vietnam. He believed that Communism was a black evil that should be stopped. He believed that the United States as a country was sincerely trying to help the Vietnamese just as much as he was personally trying to help them by repairing and sewing up some of their broken and bloodied bodies, and if half of the people in this country failed to understand that then it was a tragedy for all of them. Where his work was concerned Keller was not an emotional man, because emotion could waste away the energy he needed to save lives. In the operating theatre a patient was just a square of organs in need of repair as seen through the cut-away section of a green, operating sheet. It had to be that way if he was to work calmly and objectively, but today his equilibrium was unbalanced. He had lost one of this morning's patients because he had been forced to hurry, because they were coming in too fast and there was no time. To restore that balance he had allowed himself to acknowledge the three lives he had saved; he had no reason to be ashamed of his work here, and he saw no reason to deny his birthright. He could no more have hidden behind the false image of pretending to be English than he could have hidden physically behind the Vietnamese nurse who had tried to bar his way.

"My name is Doctor Richard Keller," he told the young Viet Cong leader, looking down into the fiercely hostile eyes. "And I am an American."

He pointed directly to Mary and added:

"This girl is English — but I am American."

The young guerrilla curled his finger closer about the trigger of his combat rifle and the nervous tension that was bottled up inside him seemed ready to explode into murder, but his eyes flickered for a moment to Thi Xin.

"How many more Americans are here?"

"There are no more." The Vietnamese girl was wringing her hands together, like the white wings of two small birds trying to strangle each other. "This is a civilian hospital, for Vietnamese civilians. We have one American doctor and one English nurse, they are volunteers. The rest of our staff are all Vietnamese. All of our patients are Vietnamese."

The long-haired youth looked at Keller again and said coldly:

"We have orders to kill all Americans. We have orders to kill all foreign interventionists."

"Your orders refer to American soldiers," Thi Xin insisted. "Here there is only one American doctor. He has no weapons. He is only here to help us. These patients are our people! We need more doctors!"

The young guerrilla hesitated and then looked back to his companions. They were all of his own age and their faces were blank as they awaited his lead. Finally he snapped at them:

"Stay here and keep guard. I will see if there are any more Americans. "

He pushed rudely past Keller and began to walk slowly down the length of the ward. He stared into each cot with its three or four frightened child faces, and at the squatting black-gowned old women. No one spoke to him, and even the children in agony who habitually whimpered or cried were silent. The squalor and the helplessness of the tiny wasted and bandaged bodies impressed him, but when he reached the end of the ward he was still not quite satisfied. He pushed open the far door through which Keller had entered and passed into the men's ward beyond.

Mary, Keller and Thi Xin all remembered in the same moment that Rene Chauvel still occupied the first bed in that next ward. Thi Xin had been caught out once in a lie, and now she wrung her hands more tightly as her eyes dilated with fear, for she knew that it would be impossible to convince the young Viet Cong that Chauvel was not another American.

******

Chauvel had been awake when the American surgeon had walked past his bed to enter the children's ward, and before the door had swung shut he had heard the sharp challenge of the young Viet Cong. The one hostile word and the sounds of gunfire that echoed distantly all around the city were enough to give him an inkling of what was happening. He tried to sit up, but as he lifted his shoulders from the bed there was a deep, piercing pain in his stomach just above the

186

groin. While he lay still he was reasonably comfortable, but he could not bend his body forward.

He gritted his teeth and tried to hear what was happening, but now the door into the next ward was closed and he could only catch the faint mutter of voices. The conscious patients in his ward who were in a position to see through the glass panels of the dividing doors were silent, but they were craning their necks and looking at each other with worried eyes. There was no one here who could speak French or English and Chauvel cursed under his breath. He pushed back the single sheet that covered him, more to protect him from the flies than anything else because the heat was sweaty and oppressive, and cautiously he moved his body again. He had to find out what was happening for himself, but this time he stayed flat and swiveled carefully on his buttocks to bring his head and shoulders closer to the door. He succeeded in twisting his body round by some thirty degrees, and then with his left elbow almost slipping off the edge of the bed he eased up his shoulders by six inches and turned his head. He saw a fleeting glimpse of the children's ward through the windows of the closed door and then he had to fall back. The pain was like being knifed all over again.

During those few seconds he had seen Keller standing with his back towards him at the far end of the ward, and beyond Keller the pale faces of the two nurses and then the five guerrillas with their leveled combat rifles. He had seen that the Vietnamese nurse was arguing and trying to reason with the intruders but that was all.

Gritting his teeth again Chauvel wondered what if anything he could do to help them, and then he remembered the 0.45 Colt automatic that had been in his jacket pocket. His clothes were stuffed into the small locker beside his bed, and if the policemen who had brought him in had been too busy to search him then perhaps the gun would still be there. Chauvel swiveled his body back until he was laying full length along the bed once more, and then he allowed his left arm to hang over the edge of the bed and reached back for the door of the locker. The stitches in his arm pulled and gave him fresh pain, but it was not as excruciating as the pain in his stomach, which was perhaps why he had not noticed it before. He found the catch on the locker and pulled it open, and then fumbled inside for his clothes. The first item he found was his trousers and he dropped them in disgust. Then he found the heavier cloth of his jacket and dragged it free. The weight gave him cause to hope and he lifted the jacket on to the bed beside him. The right hand pocket bulged and at one end of the bulge was a neat but blackened hole in the material. Chauvel moved his right hand across his chest and pulled the automatic free. The jacket he dropped beside his trousers.

He was sweating now and he listened with the Colt cocked ready in his hand. He could still hear the mutter of voices and he had to take another look into the next ward.

He steeled himself against the pain and shifted his weight to the very edge of the bed. Then he began to swivel his body again but this time bring, his legs out of the bed. As they swung slowly down to the floor he used his arms to press his upper body away from the bed, struggling to sit up without the necessity of bending at the waist. He succeeded despite the fire in his belly which threatened to burn out his mind with black flames, and the sweat began to drip from his face. He was not sure of what he intended to do next, but when he looked through into the next ward he saw the black-haired guerrilla leader walking slowly towards him with the oiled and polished combat rifle balanced precisely in his hands. The young Viet Cong was examining each bed as he passed, and so failed to see the fair head and blue eyes of the Frenchman watching him through the glass.

Chauvel knew that within a moment the youth would enter this ward, and one 0.45 Colt would be no match for five Ak-47 Chinese rifles. The automatic could only be a last resort.

Instinct told Chauvel that if he was discovered here then his presence could only make matters worse for Keller and his two nurses. He looked around his bed but there was only one possible place of concealment. Just in front of him there was a tall broom cupboard against the wall behind the door, and although there would not be enough room to get inside he could prop himself behind it in the corner of the wall. He pushed himself upright from the bed and almost drowned in sweat and pain, but he retained his automatic and sufficient strength of mind to kick his incriminating clothes under the bed and out of sight. He lurched over to the wall and turned his body so that he jammed his shoulders into the corner. He had to fight hard to brace his legs and prevent himself from slipping down, and then with his left hand he opened the door of the broom cupboard and pulled it back to form a screen in front of his body. With a final effort he kept the Colt steady in his hand.

The door from the children's ward was pushed open and the young Viet Cong came through. He paused for a moment, as nervous and as dangerous as a jungle animal, and the combat rifle moved in a half circle as his eyes scanned the ward. He looked at the empty bed that Chauvel had just left, but it did not seem to arouse his suspicions. Walking softly he moved further into the ward, and began to inspect the patients.

Chauvel watched him above the top line of the broom cupboard door, and he knew that his own position could be betrayed by any one of the other patients who had silently watched his movements. However, to betray him would also have betrayed Keller and the two nurses, and would have started a gun battle in which too many people could have died. The silence was maintained. It was a fragile silence, like a tangible thing suspended by the most delicate of threads, but it held. No one spoke to the young Viet Cong; no one greeted him or cursed him. They merely watched him approach and then avoided his searching eyes.

The youth stopped suddenly and wrinkled his nose. His flat face creased in an expression of disgust and Chauvel realized that he had got his first whiff of the poor devil dying from the perforated ulcer. It was a sick, nauseous, death smell and it was too much for the young guerrilla. He turned away as suddenly as he had stopped and Chauvel was only just in time in with-drawing his blonde head back below the level of his screen. The Viet Cong walked briskly with one hand to his nose and hurried back into the children's ward.

******

Keller and the two nurses watched him return. He stopped in front of them and glared at Thi Xin.

"This place stinks," he told her. "And we are needed elsewhere to fight for the liberation. You may carry on with your work."

He pushed past them and his companions turned to leave, but then he hesitated for a moment to glare even more ferociously at Keller. If he had found this hated member of the alien race in any other circumstances he would not have hesitated to march him outside and have him shot, but he had seen the suffering and the need for a doctor within these walls, and there still existed that thin dividing line between a patriot and a mere assassin.

"American!" he said again.

And then he spat in disgust at Keller's feet and walked out.

Mary and Thi Xin stared at each other, and when the intruders had gone they ran into the next ward. They stopped and looked down at the empty bed, and then the door of the broom cupboard creaked and swung back into place. Chauvel swayed towards them with his eyes closed and the automatic in his hand pointing limply at the floor, and they caught him before he fell.

CHAPTER TWELVE

On the fifth day after her death Phat Sang was buried, hastily and cheaply and without ceremony, and in company with a dozen other unclaimed corpses from the hospital mortuary. It was the only positive thing that the South Vietnamese Government had ever done for her, and in that she was lucky. At that time many of the war dead of Saigon and Cholon lay rotting in the streets because no one dared to risk getting shot merely to collect bodies. There was no time for tears, and for Phat Sang there was no one to shed them. Her passing went almost unnoticed, although Chin the Chinese bar girl eventually searched the streets for her in vain, and she did qualify for a pencil mark on the impressive reels of statistics. And why should she have been noticed? She was just one of many, many thousands of lost refugees. When giant political ideologies fought for their greater glories there was no time for the Phat Sangs of this world, they had to be assigned to their proper place, which was the limbo of irrelevancy. Glory be to God and the American Dream! Glory be to Mao Tse Tung and the Red Gods of Marx and Lenin! And death and misery to the little Phat Sangs.

She was born, she lived, she died, all too quickly; or perhaps not quickly enough: and all that she left behind was her handbag containing the picture of Mom and Pop in Ohio, discarded and hidden by rubbish in a gutter, and her new-born daughter who was carefully tended by an English nurse. The little girl was healthy despite her violent and premature entry into the world, and despite the burn scar of the bullet that was her birthmark. Her skin was almost white, and although she had the flat forehead and the narrow eyes of a Vietnamese the eyes themselves were a light hazel in color. She was a very pretty little baby, although obviously a half caste, and occasionally Mary wondered who her father might have been. Because the Americans were so predominant she could only guess that the baby's father must have been an American.

******

The bloody battle for Saigon was brought to its lingering end, and on the tenth day after the terror had been unleashed Mary stopped at Chauvel's bedside to tell him that he was to be moved.

"The worst is over," she said. "And tomorrow there'll be an ambulance to transfer you to the American hospital. I'm afraid they've been busy too, and this is the first opportunity we've had. "

"Please do not apologize, Mademoiselle, you have looked after me very well." Chauvel smiled and added: "But can you spare another of your valuable minutes to talk with me. For a journalist it is very difficult to be in a position where he is surrounded by great events, and yet still be out of touch with the news."

Mary shrugged and said: "It's still all very confusing." And then she smiled because she had given him the same answer so many times before. She tried to be more explicit and went on: "The Government radio station was burned down, but according to the reports we hear over the military radio, the Americans and the South Vietnamese forces control most of the city. They say they've cleaned out the Viet Cong, although they admit that the Viet Cong still have influence in seven out of the city's nine precincts, and the Viet Cong still have their stronghold in precinct five, that's the area of Cholon with the biggest percentage of Chinese population. In this area they've been driven back."

She paused and then added: "According to the stories we've heard from our out-patients the Viet Cong have murdered a lot of women and children, but only the wives and children of Army officers and people like that. Wherever possible they've spared ordinary civilians, and I've heard that ordinary soldiers in the South Vietnamese Army have even been allowed to pass through the Viet Cong lines to visit their families. They just have to go unarmed. It's total war and yet it isn't. That's what makes it so confusing."

"There is a pattern," Chauvel explained. "The Viet Cong policy is to be selective in their killing, whereas the sheer weight of American bombing and fire-power is anything but selective. The Americans have made too many mistakes and bombed too many friendly villages, and everybody knows that the American Air Force is responsible for more civilian deaths and property destroyed than any other factor. The facts prove themselves, and are a great asset to the Viet Cong in winning them national loyalty in the countryside. I am afraid that although the American Air Force would undoubtedly be supremely effective in destroying an enemy nation and winning a declared conventional war, it is nothing but a useless liability in attempting to create a political peace."

"Perhaps you should have been a politician," Mary said.

"God forbid," Chauvel replied. "Then nobody could believe a word that I say."

Mary smiled and made him lift his head while she punched the shape back into his pillow, and her smile was a warm and refreshing glimpse of sunshine.

"You are not so weary now," Chauvel observed. "That is good."

Mary nodded. "The pressure is off, but now we have a new kind of worry. Over the past ten days the refuse has been rotting in the streets with no one to clear it away, and now it is attracting the rats which are beginning to thrive. If you go outside the hospital you can smell the stink where people are pouring petrol over their rubbish and trying to burn it. We have had to do the same in the back yard — and of course we have to fear epidemics of cholera or even the plague. The conditions are ripe and in the casualty department we've been giving mass inoculations to everyone we can reach. That was the injection you had yesterday."

Chauvel touched the sore spot on his arm and asked:

"If an epidemic breaks out can you control it?"

"It is difficult to say. This is the beginning of the plague season in Saigon when the rats carry the biggest number of fleas. The rats thrive in the grain and rice warehouses and of course the fleas thrive with them, and then the grain sacks get distributed all over the country. In 1965 there were over four thousand cases of plague reported in Vietnam. It's just one of the side issues of war."

Chauvel grimaced, the idea of dying from bubonic plague was not attractive and he changed the subject.

"What is happening outside of Saigon, to the other cities that were attacked in the Tet Offensive?"

Mary frowned. "The Americans say that the Viet Cong have been driven back into the jungles, and that thousands of them were killed. The Viet Cong were only really successful here and in Hue. Here they've been almost cleared out, and although they're still holding on to Hue I think it must be only a matter of time before they have to fall back."

"Did they take Khe Sanh?"

"The marine base near Laos, no, they haven't attacked it yet, but the Americans are still afraid that they might."

Chauvel was thoughtful for a moment, and then he said:

"Now I don't think that there is any need, or any point. For the Americans Dienbienphu was right here in Saigon. Khe Sanh was only their queen, and Giap has checkmated their king."

Mary said slowly, "I don't understand."

"It is over," Chauvel said gravely. "The struggle for Vietnam is over. Let me explain, Mademoiselle Mary, that in the last two weeks we have seen the final phase of Mao Tse Tung's theory for waging a successful revolutionary war. The formula takes three steps. First the build up of secret guerrilla cells which increase their own morale and their own supplies of weapons and ammunition by means of ambush and hit and run attacks, which at the same time decreases the morale and resources of the enemy. Second is the gradual build up of regular forces which can meet and defeat the enemy on even terms. And the third and final stage is to overtake the enemy in strength and morale and then carry the war from the jungle in an invasion of his cities. The Viet Gong have now pushed the war and that formula to its ultimate limit, but they have been repelled in the final phase."

"Then the Americans have won."

"No, Mademoiselle, the Americans lost this war long before they started. The Viet Cong had won the political war before they arrived, the Americans could only hope to win a military war, and they have lost that also because they could not win it. I said that Giap had played checkmate, but let me correct myself, it is now a game of perpetual check. The Americans cannot take the countryside, they have known that for a long while, and that is why President Johnson has been crying out for peace talks over the past few months. The Communists have ignored him because they believed that they could still win a military victory with stage three of the Mao formula. They have failed and they must realize now that they will never take the cities. There is nothing left for either side except to accept that they must talk a compromise peace."

Mary had work to do, but she was intrigued by his line of reasoning and she prompted him to go on.

"Then you think that after all this they will finally sit down and hold peace talks?"

"I am certain," Chauvel said. "I think that President Johnson will have to resign. Vietnam was a major blunder in American foreign policy, and their historians of the future will need a scapegoat; and of course the man who escalated the war to its limit can hardly be the man to talk a sincere and convincing desire for peace."

Chauvel paused and then went on bitterly: "Yes, Mademoiselle, the war is over, but the battles will go on. War is like a living thing that dies in spasms of violence, and there will be no full stop to the fighting for many months, perhaps many years to come. In the meantime the politicians will merely talk of peace. They will argue like petty, nauseous little children over where the talks are to be held, and who sits at which end of the table, and who speaks first, and who committed the worst atrocities in the past. They will play the peace talks for maximum propaganda and seek to accuse each other and whitewash themselves. And in between their noble press statements and their heroic efforts to save their own stupid personal and national faces and reputations they will drink champagne and eat caviar and emit pompous platitudes of self praise. And while this sick and disgusting spectacle drags itself on and on and on men will still be fighting and dying in the mud and blood of the swamps and jungles of Vietnam. This is what happened after the fall of Dienbienphu, and I cannot see that the political leaders of this world have changed. All the gallons of blood spilled during the coming peace talks will be held as nothing compared to the saving of political face."

It was an emotional outburst, and Mary did not know that he had lived through the hell of the Viet Minh prison camps while the former peace talks had been held in Geneva. She felt that perhaps she should not excite him, and yet she was interested in what he had to say.

"I suppose," she said uncertainly," that the result is a draw, but how can they compromise?"

"One thing seems clear," Chauvel answered. "The Americans will have to withdraw. The North Vietnamese will do the same, but the Viet Cong are the South Vietnamese, they cannot withdraw because this is their home. They will have to take a part in the Government of this country, and although the Americans may save their own faces with a paper peace the Communists will take over after they have gone. Then will come the Land Reform Campaigns and the trials, and another wave of bloodshed with another million people purged, and only then will the guerrilla fighters begin to understand that they have been used. I can see no happy ending for Vietnam."

Mary shuddered. "Will Communism take over all of Asia?" she asked. "Is it unbeatable?"

Chauvel thought for a moment and then said carefully:

"To a large extent that still depends upon the Americans. Their mistake in Vietnam lay in the belief that all the Asian countries were just a set of identical dominoes, and that if one country fell to Communism then they must all fall. But the countries of Asia are not dominoes; they all have their own individual history and heritage. The history of Vietnam, and Laos which must fall with it, was a history of bloody mismanagement and oppression by French colonialism, which left Communism their only heritage. The other countries of South East Asia do not have that past, or the desire to become Communist."

"What about Cambodia?" Mary objected. "Cambodia was also a part of the old French empire of Indo-China."

"That is true," Chauvel admitted. "But Cambodia has been granted a reprieve period of transition which has allowed it to develop into a free kingdom. Prince Sihanouk has managed to keep his country neutral and has achieved fourteen years of peace while Vietnam and Laos have bled and burned. I think that as the Americans withdraw from Vietnam so Sihanouk will be forced to flirt more openly with the Communist world, he cannot afford to be on hostile terms with his Communist neighbors. However, if he can stay in power and continues to walk the neutral tightrope, then Cambodia could become a kind of Yugoslavia in reverse; a free nation friendly to the Communist world which can act as a buffer between the two sides. The danger in Cambodia lies in the Cambodian Generals who could be tempted to stage a military coup. Generals become frustrated when they are not allowed to justify their existence by waging war — especially when it is an American-backed war which will enable them to make their personal fortunes out of dollar aid. Sihanouk has very prudently withdrawn his troops from his eastern border regions where the Viet Cong have their sanctuaries, but although this has meant peace for Cambodia it has not pleased the Cambodian Generals, or the American Generals who would prefer to widen the war. No General likes to admit defeat, and if they cannot win a war in one sphere they will willingly shift to another, regardless of the cost in blood and refugees."

Chauvel pulled a wry face and finished sadly; Cambodia is a question mark and I would not gamble on its future, but it would be a tragedy if it were to become a second Vietnam now that the struggle for the first Vietnam is for all practical purposes over. We can only hope that Sihanouk can stay in power, or that if he falls the Americans will not be foolish enough to support a new regime of military dictators."

He became gloomily silent and after a moment Mary prompted him; "What about the other countries of Asia, the countries that were not part of Indo-China."

Chauvel considered: "Thailand has always been the land of the free. Malaysia and Indonesia were colonies but they too have had sufficient time to find an independent freedom. None of them desire Communism, and they do need the American umbrella. A new line will have to be drawn where the old line should have been drawn — down the natural line of the Mekong."

"That's a very long line," Mary pointed out doubtfully.

"I agree, but it is a wide, natural line, and there are no bridges across the Mekong. It divides the old French empire which is a lost cause from the free kingdom of Thailand which welcomes the American presence and cannot associate them with western colonialism. It would be another tragedy if the United States were to desert the whole of Asia simply because they have received a bloody nose in the one corner where they were not wanted."

Chauvel smiled suddenly and continued: "Perhaps I should be telling all this to Doctor Keller and not to you, or better still to one of the top brass Generals here in Vietnam, except that the American Generals make a practice of never listening to anyone except the "top men" of their own rank, who usually know the least and have the most reasons for presenting a false picture. However, I would hope that the Americans have learned some lessons in Vietnam. By now they must have realized that it is the height of folly to support a group of corrupt military dictators simply because they profess to be anti-communist, and they must have realized that their military machine cannot crush a Communist insurgency at ground level in a country such as this."

"Then how do you stop it?" Mary asked practically.

"The answer is very simple, although it may not be so in practice. Communism can only breed on two things, poverty and ignorance. It succeeded in Tsarist Russia, in war and famine-stricken China, and in French-oppressed Vietnam, because the ordinary people were broken down to dirt level and had nothing to lose. By the standards they had before they have even gained. If the rest of Asia is to be saved then the standard of living for the average peasant must be raised until he has something to lose, and his standard of education must be raised so that he can understand the alternatives. Then a Communist insurgency will have no roots on which to grow, and the people themselves will be prepared to resist any physical invasion from outside by Red China or Red Vietnam."

"You mean that to preserve the rest of Asia from Communism the United States and the West have to give the people a better deal than Communism can offer?"

"Precisely, and the same applies to Africa and South America. Noble talk of democratic freedom means nothing to a starving peasant. First give him a full belly and a comfortable life in which he retains his self respect, and then he will appreciate democratic freedom. But remember that each country has its own national pride, heritage and culture; they will resist becoming mere American satellites."

Mary said quietly: "You make it sound as though there is hope for the world, even yet. But what happens to the poor devils who are already slaves in the Communist police states?"

"Communism defeats its own ends," Chauvel pointed out wryly. "The Communist leaders have to keep some of their promises and raise standards of living and education, and when they do that they widen minds and bring about the start of their own downfall. In Russia life is drab, but the people are comfortable and well-educated. The Stalin era is over and the police state is more relaxed, only the intellectuals really suffer. The Soviet society has to become less severe if it is to avoid another internal explosion - and remain whole. Asian Communism must eventually start on the same trend, if it survives after Comrade Mao dies. In one or two hundred years there will perhaps be no Communism as we know it now and perhaps no United States of America. The world map will be re-drawn. "

He smiled and finished: "There is never hope, and yet there is always hope. There is never change, and yet there is always change. In one hundred or two hundred years there will be new empires, new power blocs, new ideologies, and perhaps new gods — and the old wars. That is conflict. That is life."

"And that is also your minute," Mary said firmly. She glanced at her wristwatch. "I have some work to do."

******

Later that afternoon Chauvel received a visit from Suzanne. She had come daily over the past three or four days since the area around the hospital had been declared relatively safe, insisting that she could stay away from him for no longer. He looked forward to her visits and after she had kissed him warmly he told her that he was now considered well enough to be moved. For the first few days Harvey had accompanied her and had appeared briefly to say hello before waiting in the reception hall, but today Suzanne was alone.

"What's happened to Bill?" Chauvel asked her.

"He's busy," Suzanne said. "And the city isn't so dangerous now. I couldn't impose on him to act as my escort for ever. "

"You came in a taxi alone?"

Suzanne shook her head. "No, I have our little Renault car. The police found it in the street where you left it and brought it back to the hotel yesterday. They said that we were very lucky that the Viet Hong did not burn it, or turn it over to use as a part of one of their barricades."

Chauvel was thoughtful while they talked of other things through the rest of her visit, and when it was time for her to leave he mentioned the car again.

"Suzanne, do something for me, please. Call for a taxi to take you home and leave the Renault here at the hospital. You can leave the keys with me."

Her eyes were doubtful and puzzled.

"But why?"

"Mademoiselle Mary and her Vietnamese friend have a transport problem." Chauvel explained how they had come to lose their bicycles and then went on carefully: "Now that it is safe for them to return to their home at night Madame Phuong has to drive then to their apartment and then collect them again in the mornings with the hospital Land Rover. It is an inconvenient arrangement, but although Mademoiselle Mary can drive the Land Rover could be needed here during the night. I think that to solve their problem and show my gratitude I will let them borrow the Renault for a few weeks — until they can get themselves new bicycles, and while I shall not be well enough to use the car anyway. You can use a taxi to visit me at the American hospital when I am moved, and I would prefer that the rest of the time you stayed inside the hotel."

Suzanne believed him and made no argument, for it was only in the side arrangements of her sex life that she made a habit of opposing his wishes. She gave him the keys, kissed him again and said goodbye. After she had gone Chauvel weighed the keys in his hand and reflected that perhaps it would be a nice gesture to let Mary Francis borrow the car, but first he needed it for a purpose of his own.

He had a score to settle with Vu Phan Quang.

CHAPTER THIRTEEN

Chauvel lay quietly through the hours that remained of the afternoon, although several times he glanced at his wristwatch. The hands showed six fifteen when at last he decided to move, for he wanted to time his arrival at Quang's villa as close as possible to the curfew hour of seven o'clock, when it would be getting dark and he could be certain of finding his enemy at home. He waited until there were no nurses in the ward and then very gingerly he sat up. His stomach wound had healed well, although he could still feel pain if he moved too sharply. He sat on the edge of the bed and pulled off his pajama jacket, and then began to don his shirt which he took from his bedside locker.

Getting out of his pajama trousers was simple, he just stood up and let them drop, but pulling on his ordinary trousers gave him some difficulty. He had to bend a little to pull them on and his face tightened with a wince of pain. He zipped the fly and then fastened his belt only loosely, and then sat on the bed again to struggle with his shoes and socks. He managed that task also, although afterwards he felt like sitting still for a few minutes until he was breathing more easily again. However, he wanted to get out without being seen and could not afford the delay. He stood up and put on his jacket, and checked that the Colt automatic was back in his pocket. The Colt was the magic, phallic symbol of power that would, more than make up for his physical weakness when he faced Quang. He smiled grimly and then picked up the keys of the Renault from beneath his pillow.

He started to leave just as Mary Francis walked into the ward, and for the first time since his arrival Chauvel was not pleased to see her. He cursed silently under his breath. Mary had finished work and was looking for Thi Xin, but when she saw Chauvel standing fully dressed beside his bed she stopped. They stared at each other and then her face adopted a brisk, no-nonsense expression instead, of its customary smile.

"What on earth do you think you're doing?" she demanded. "You shouldn't be out of bed."

"I am sorry, Mademoiselle," Chauvel apologized quietly. "But I am leaving."

Mary walked up to him and folded her arms, barring his way and unperturbed by the fact that he was a good seven inches talker than her own five foot three.

"Monsieur Chauvel," she said firmly. "You are not leaving until tomorrow. Please take your clothes off and get back into bed."

Chauvel looked around the overcrowded ward where all eyes were watching them curiously. Every drama here was a public one, but he had become accustomed to that.

"I think that there are worse cases in need of my bed," he said. "I have occupied it for too long."

"But there's an ambulance coming for you tomorrow."

"I know, but I have decided that I will not go to another hospital. Even the American hospital will be crowded, and now that I am fit to stand I can go back to my hotel. My wife will take care of me."

"But you are not fit to stand."

Chauvel smiled wryly and held up his hands to show that he needed no support.

"But I am standing," he pointed out.

Mary looked exasperated.

"Why didn't you say that you wanted to go back to your hotel when your wife was here? Perhaps we could have allowed her to take you home."

Chauvel had been hoping that she would not ask that question, and the only answer that he could make was the truth.

"I have some private business that I must perform. That will not take me long but it must be finished first."

"You're not fit for any private business," Mary argued. "Whatever it is, it can wait."

"It has already waited too long," Chauvel said grimly, and with feeling.

Mary stared at him uncertainly.

"Mademoiselle," Chauvel said more quietly. "It is only my body that is still weak. I assure you that there is nothing wrong with my mind. And this is an important matter. Will you call a taxi for me?"

Mary hesitated, and then decided that to keep him here she needed reinforcements. Either Keller or Doctor Phuong would carry more authority than her own, and would have the medical knowledge to convince Chauvel in more precise terms that he was acting foolishly. She relaxed her arms and then nodded, for in her profession a little white lie was sometimes necessary.

"Alright, Monsieur Chauvel, sit down on the bed for a few minutes and wait while I go to the telephone."

Chauvel smiled gratefully and sat down, and then Mary hurried out of the ward. Chauvel gave her a few seconds to get clear and then sighed regretfully because he had to deceive her. He knew that he had very little time before she found one of the doctors and he hurried out through the children's ward and the back exit.

******

When Mary returned with Keller two minutes later they found the bed empty, but one of the Vietnamese patients simply pointed through the children's ward to show them which way Chauvel had gone. They hurried

213

through to the back yard, and then circled hopefully round to the front entrance and the main street. There was no sign of the Frenchman, and although it was still daylight and there were a large number of people passing to and fro the language barrier prevented them from asking any questions. Mary gazed around helplessly, and Keller shrugged his shoulders.

"He must have been lucky," Keller said. "He must have found a taxi almost immediately. He's a fool, but there's not much that we can do about it now — except hope that his luck holds, and that he doesn't do anything to burst open those stitches."

Mary knew that Keller was right, and that they could not waste time in searching for a patient who was at least capable of walking out of the hospital. With their Vietnamese patients it happened often when they decided that they were cured or incurable or had private affairs to attend. It was just one of the frustrations which as westerners they had to learn to take in their stride. Mary was angry for she realized now that Chauvel had tricked her, but she was still concerned for his welfare. As she walked back into the hospital with Keller she said:

"I think I'd better telephone his wife, I still have their number at the Continental Hotel. He'll probably turn up there eventually, and she'll have to try and keep him confined to bed until he's really well."

"A sound idea," Keller agreed. "Give her the telephone number of the American hospital. Then if he does turn up needing medical attention she can call them to come and fetch him." He grimaced and repeated for the second time, "The man's a fool."

******

While Mary made the telephone call to Suzanne, Chauvel was driving the little Renault saloon slowly back into Saigon. The flow of traffic had not yet resumed its normal race-track speed and torrent proportions, for the large mass of the population was still scared and in hiding behind closed doors, and for that he was glad. Every time that he had to use the brake or clutch a stab of pain thrust through his groin and he doubted whether he would have been capable of driving the car under the normal conditions. It was becoming dusk and he could have driven faster, but he wanted to time his arrival at the villa just right so that he had the cover of darkness. He turned north before he reached the central market and headed out into the suburbs, and twice he had to stop and check his way with the street map in the dashboard locker of the car. He had never visited Quang's villa, but he knew the location and the address.

When he reached the area he drove more slowly for there were many signs of war damage. This was a purely residential suburb with mostly luxury or semi-luxury homes, and now it seemed quiet and deserted. Only a few of the once-smart villas showed lights, and through the deepening shadows Chauvel could see a large number of smashed and gaping windows, and bullet scars clipped out of the pink and yellow-washed walls. The broken fronds from decapitated palms littered the roads, and in places the lower walls surrounding the villa gardens had been reduced to rubble. Obviously the Viet Cong had hit this suburb hard and it looked as though most of the residents had fled. Chauvel was wary of meeting a police or army patrol, for he guessed that they must be lurking somewhere to keep a watch for looters.

He stopped the Renault in a side street a hundred yards away from Quang's home, and parked it without lights in the deep patch of shadow thrown by the palm trees that lined the edge of the pavement. The time was seven o'clock, curfew hour and dark enough for his purpose. He checked the magazine of the Colt automatic, from which only one shot had been fired, and he was satisfied. He got out on to the pavement and locked the car, and with his right hand and the gun resting in his jacket pocket he walked slowly back to the main road and turned towards Quang's villa. He kept close to the wall, and although the pain in his groin was gradually increasing and his muscles had the substance of jelly he felt sure that he could finish the job that he had come to do. The Colt automatic was his strength, plus that old but invaluable element of surprise.

Chauvel did not know Quang very well, except as a shadowy figure in the background with whom he had been sharing his wife, He knew the Vietnamese mostly by reputation, and by instinct from their first brief meetings six years before when he had tried unsuccessfully to cultivate the politician as a news source. In recent years they had not met at all, for Suzanne had been very careful to keep them apart, but Chauvel felt that he knew Quang's mentality only too well. Quang had been warned that he had a jealous husband to contend with, and one who was grimly contemplating murder, and so he had made his own murder attempt first. He had failed, and now he would be expecting a return attempt on his own life. Chauvel knew that Quang could not have survived so long in Vietnamese politics without taking every possible precaution for his own self-preservation, and thinking at least one step ahead of his opponents. Therefore it was only logical to suspect that Quang would keep a careful watch on the progress of the jealous husband he had tried to have murdered, and that he would ensure that he had sufficient warning to be prepared when that jealous husband was discharged from hospital.

Chauvel knew that he had to think at least two moves ahead of his shrewd and unscrupulous enemy, and by discharging himself from the hospital while he was still unfit he hoped to evade whatever warning system Quang had devised, even if it included his own wife. Also he needed to act while the city was still recovering from turmoil, and while there were still enough Viet Cong stubbornly clinging on to their positions to make another violent death by shooting pass unsuspected.

Slowly but confidently Chauvel approached the villa, but when he arrived he cursed softly under his breath. Through a broken gap in the garden wall he stepped on to a mangled flower bed and he stared for a moment at the shell-smashed ruins. He drew the Colt from his pocket but it was an unnecessary gesture for the smell of death was already ripe in the air.

He held his breath and moved forward, and as he circled round the gardens he observed that the front entrance to the villa had been blasted open, and that almost half the building was demolished. For ten days the men who had died there had lain unburied, and it was obvious that no one could be alive inside. Chauvel backed off and wondered whether Quang and his family were among the bodies, but he did not have the stomach to search through the ruins and check all the rotted corpses. A black crow flew from the palm fronds in the corner of the garden and made him start with alarm, and then he went back to the main road. It was night now and the villa was like a stark, fallen tomb in a graveyard, and he hurried back to his car.

For a few minutes he sat motionless inside the Renault, resting both hands on the wheel and staring blankly down the side street that stretched ahead, thinking. On the face of it the Viet Cong had attacked the villa and accomplished his job for him, but Chauvel could not convince himself that Quang was dead. It was too simple and Quang was not the kind of man to sit in a trap until it closed. He was a Government minister and his home was an obvious target, equally obviously he would make a point of not being at home when the Viet Cong called.

Chauvel pondered and decided that if Quang had moved out before the attack then there was only one place where he would be likely to run for cover, and that was the apartment in central Saigon where he had so often entertained Suzanne. Straightening his shoulders Chauvel started the engine of the Renault, and decided that the love nest apartment would be an even more fitting place to kill Quang if he was there.

He backed the car out on to the main road and then drove back towards the city. He was gritting his teeth now against the deepening stabs of pain in his stomach and concentrating on his driving and finding his way, and then he was electrified by a faint bang in the sky as the empty and darkened streets were flooded with glaring white light.

He was so startled that he almost crashed the car, but then he realized what was happening. It was after curfew and either the police or the Army were firing parachute flares over the still contested areas of the city to deny the remnants of the Viet Cong the advantages of attack offered by the night. It made him aware again of the danger of running into a patrol, for now they would be certain to shoot on sight at anything that moved. He clenched his jaws more tightly and began to drive even faster through the empty streets.

Perhaps he was lucky, or perhaps the police were merely making gestures and fighting a war of nerves, for although more parachute flares burst at intervals overhead he encountered no patrols or barricades. He left the suburbs behind and drove straight to the apartment, and again he found an adjacent side street where he could park the car out of sight. Here all was again quiet and dark, and he got out on to the pavement and slipped his right hand into his jacket pocket to grip the butt of his automatic. He winced as he stepped away from the car, and now he was walking very slowly indeed as he made his way back to the main boulevard and turned towards Quang's secondary home.

There were no lights behind Quang's window, but that meant nothing for there were no lights anywhere. The whole population of Saigon, except for the homeless, was hidden and listening in the darkness of their rooms, like a race of human ostriches praying that because they could not see they could not be seen. Chauvel had passed some groups of refugees sleeping or squatting with their chattels on the pavements, but here he was alone. He glanced across the road to the cafe-restaurant where he had once sat and watched for Suzanne to come out, and reflected wryly that he was in an even weaker state now than he had been then, except that now he had the gun.

He reached the door from which Suzanne had emerged on that occasion. He did not expect it to be unbolted but to his surprise it opened to his touch. He pushed, and then entered the darkness beyond, and waited until his eyes had become accustomed to the gloom and he could faintly distinguish the stairs leading up to the landing on the upper floor. He listened and could hear nothing, and yet he sensed that he was not alone. No crack of light showed above and yet the hairs prickled on the back of his neck, and he felt as though the whole building was listening in turn for him to make the first move He could not be certain that Quang was there, but if he was then tonight one of them must die. The Greek tragedy had been written long before, and only this last act had to be performed.

Chauvel began to climb the stairs, slowly because of the pain in his stomach, and because it was imperative that he made no noise. He pulled the Colt automatic from his pocket and with his free hand felt his way along the wall. He did not feel like an intending assassin or murderer, because he had been trained as a soldier, as a paratrooper of the Legion, and as he had told Suzanne, he had killed better men than Quang at Dienbienphu, and at Hoa Binh, and at Long San, and a score of other place names that would ring for ever in the dead notes of French military glory. Tonight he would kill not to order and for duty, but because he had made a vow, because it was the only possible way of resolving his wife's infidelity, because it was the only logical way to protect himself from a second murder attempt, and because Vu Phan Quang was only fit for killing.

For tonight's work the moralists and the law-makers would condemn him, because no politician or General had started the chain of command to sanction the death of Vu Phan Quang. Fourteen years before they had applauded his slaughter of the gallant little freedom fighters of the Viet Minh, but Quang who was corrupt and selfish and obsessed with his own survival and greed was smart enough to proclaim himself an anti-Communist and as such was technically on the side of God and the angels and beyond retribution. Tonight Rene Chauvel would be a murderer, but he was thinking for himself, and he was prepared to accept the responsibility in any afterworld for his own actions, and he no longer cared a damn for the moralists and the law-makers. His mind and his soul were strong enough to bear his own conscience.

He reached the landing and quietly felt his way around in the darkness. There was only one door facing him and very gingerly he turned the doorknob with his left hand. The knob turned silently but when he pushed the door resisted his carefully applied weight and he knew that it must be locked. It was no more than he had expected and he released the knob without noise and stepped back. He had come without any plan except to confront Quang before the Vietnamese could become aware that he was in any danger and now he pondered his next move. The simple way to settle the issue would be to boldly knock on the door, and then if Quang opened it to simply shoot him down. If there was no answer then he could smash the door open with one O.45 shell fired into the lock.

For a moment Chauvel hesitated, wondering whether Quang might have brought his whole family here. Then he decided that not even Quang would be coward enough to let his wife or one of his sons answer the door in his place while the city was in such a dangerous state of anarchy. Chauvel believed that no man was ever completely evil, and he suspected that even the saints must have possessed a few mild but hidden vices.

Deliberately Chauvel rapped the knuckles of his right fist hard on the door.

The echoes faded into the silence that hung like an atmosphere of petrified dread in the darkness, and then Chauvel heard a faint movement behind the closed door. There was another empty moment, as though a faint heart was steeling itself to answer, and then a voice spoke nervously in Vietnamese

."Who is there?"

"The police," Chauvel replied briskly in the same language. "We wish to talk to Monsieur Quang."

There was a shuffling sound and then the click of a switch. A faint line of light appeared at the bottom of the door and then a bolt was drawn back. Chauvel stepped one pace backwards so that he would be in shadow when the door opened and leveled his automatic. The door opened by two inches and Chauvel saw that there was a chain on the inside so that even now it could not be kicked open. Chauvel guessed that Quang would instruct him to switch on the landing light, and then peep through the crack in the door to identify his visitor, when that happened Quang would get a bullet from the automatic in his teeth.

Chauvel waited, but to his surprise there were no more precautions, and the guard chain was released. As it dropped the door was abruptly thrown wide and Chauvel blinked in the sharp burst of light. His finger tightened on the trigger but it was not Quang who faced him. Instead he was confronted by a Sergeant and two policemen in the white uniforms of the Saigon Police. He held his fire because three heavy police revolvers were lined up on the region of his navel.

The Sergeant gave him a bland, beaming smile.

"Your mistake, Monsieur Chauvel," he said. "The police are already here."

The two policemen came forward and gripped Chauvel's arms, and as their Sergeant stepped back they drew him into the room. They too were smiling as though this was a huge joke, and Chauvel made no resistance. The policemen and the Sergeant were only little men and they and their comrades were usually known to Americans and Europeans in Saigon as the White Mice, but there was nothing miniature or mouse-like about the three revolvers. The Sergeant reached forward almost apologetically and took the Colt automatic from Chauvel's hand.

"I am so sorry," he said, speaking in French. "But I must take charge of this weapon."

Chauvel said nothing. He looked beyond the Sergeant's shoulder to where Vu Phan Quang was standing placidly in the centre of the room. Quang was posed as though for a family picture with one arm around Mai Ahn and the other around his two sons. The faces of Mai Ahn and the two boys were apprehensive and uncertain, but Quang wore no expression at all. His slit eyes met Chauvel's for a moment, and he lifted his shoulders in a slight shrug. He wore his silk dressing gown with the red embroidered Chinese dragons, and managed to convey an air of unconcern and well-being. The situation was under his control, but he did not have to lift a finger. Chauvel glared at him, but then the Police Sergeant demanded his attention.

"You are, Monsieur Rene Chauvel, the press correspondent for Paris Soir?"

Chauvel looked down at him and saw no point in denying it. He was frustrated and baffled and he said angrily:

"That is correct."

"Then I am instructed to present you with this paper."

The Sergeant reached inside his tunic and produced a folded white sheet which bore several impressive official stamps and a large signature scrawled by the Chief of Police. Chauvel accepted it as though in a daze, stared at it and recognized it, and then said in disbelief:

"This is a deportation order."

"That is correct, Monsieur. You and your wife are to leave Vietnam. Two seats have been held for you on the Air France flight to Paris which leaves tomorrow afternoon."

It was so unexpected and so unreal that for the moment Chauvel forgot that technically he had been apprehended with a loaded automatic in his hand and the full intention of committing murder.

"Why?" he demanded savagely. "There's no reason — "

"We have our reasons," the Sergeant interrupted him curtly. "And you are not entitled to explanations. You will leave Vietnam and you will not return."

Chauvel looked past him again, but Quang merely moved his shoulders in another bland shrug. He was safe behind the three policemen and he was not offering explanations either. He turned and made a gesture with his hand and his two sons and Mai Ahn obediently went into the bedroom. Quang followed them and glanced back as he reached the door.

"Bon soir, Monsieur Chauvel," he said politely. "I trust that you and your wife will enjoy a pleasant flight."

CHAPTER FOURTEEN

At three o'clock the following afternoon Chauvel climbed slowly up the gangway of the waiting Air France Boeing 707 with Suzanne by his side and holding solicitously on to his elbow. He paused for a moment to take a final look around the hot run-ways of Tan Son Nhut, like rivers of molten silver that were jam-packed with military and civilian aircraft. Waiting on the feeder runways that let into the main landing strip were giant American Cargomasters and Globemasters, sleek Voodoos and Super-sabres, rows of parked helicopters and Bird Dogs, together with the dumpy black Skyraiders of Marshall Ky's Vietnamese Air Force, plus the gleaming jets of Pan Am, Cathay Pacific, and the Caravelles of Air Vietnam. It was the most efficiently organized sea of confusion in the world and fascinating to watch, but there were other passengers boarding the plane and Suzanne had to tug at Chauvel's arm to move him on. They entered the long cabin and found their seats, and Chauvel had to lower himself very carefully. He had aggravated his stomach wound so much in the past twelve hours that every movement now caused him serious pain.

He had no alternative to obeying the deportation order, for the three White Mice had escorted him back to his hotel and then called again at noon to escort him to the airport. The Sergeant and his two policemen had been firm but polite, and in view of his wound they had not hurried him unduly. The two policemen had even carried his suitcases down to the police car, and then from the police car into the airport terminal. The customs and emigration formalities had all been glossed over thanks to the presence of the Sergeant, and as Chauvel and Suzanne had passed through the final gate to the assembly point for departing passengers the three White Mice had each given them a courteous salute and had wished them: "Bon voyage!"

There had been no explanations, but only Quang could have arranged such an efficient and speedy deportation with no official reasons given, and clearly it was his influence that had ensured that they were treated with the maximum respect. Chauvel knew that he had escaped lightly only because Suzanne had to share his fate. When they were seated he turned to face her, and knowing what was coming she looked down into her lap and refused to meet his eyes.

"How did Quang know?" he asked wearily. "Who warned him to expect me last night?"

Suzanne lifted her head reluctantly, and her eyes had the soft, sorrowful look of a puppy which expected to be beaten for a crime over which there was no real control. It was a helpless look which usually saved her from the beating, and after all the years of their marriage Chauvel still believed that each time she used it she was sincere. She leaned her cheek on his shoulder and said in a low voice:

"I warned him, Rene. I had to. Mary Francis telephoned me and told me that you had left the hospital. She was worried about you. I realized what you intended to do, and why you had needed the car. I knew you still had your gun. I didn't want you to kill for me. I didn't want you to become a murderer. And I didn't want Quang to die. He was a good friend to me. I had to warn him. I knew he would think of something."

Chauvel said bitterly: "Did it occur to you that he might have thought of killing me? He could have had me shot dead just as easily as he has had me deported. I cannot imagine why he did not do so."

"It was because I asked him not to harm you," Suzanne explained simply. "Quang knows now that I love you more deeply than I could ever love anyone else, and I warned him that if he did have you killed then I would buy another gun and that when I came to kill him there would be no warning. Quang knew that I meant what I said, and he knew that he had to solve our problem in another way. That is why we are being deported."

Chauvel looked down at the wave of her dark hair, and then she turned her cheek to look up into his eyes. Her face was a beautiful, sad apology, and Chauvel was at a loss for words because he knew that she had uttered only the truth. In her heart she did love him, although with her body she would no doubt continue to betray him. For a while she would be faithful, now that he was hurt and needed her, but in the final analysis there was no solution to her excess sex urge. Because he loved her in return Chauvel could not chastise her, and so he turned his anger and frustration to the more convenient outlet of her absent lover.

"Your friend Quang is a smug and smart little bastard," he said. "But his time will come. The Americans will eventually have to leave Vietnam, they cannot afford to stay here for ever in terms of either dollars or GI blood and when they leave the Communists will take over. On that day Quang and all of his kind will be purged, and the only tragedy is that a million decent Vietnamese will be purged with them."

Suzanne disagreed. She said quietly:

"No, Rene. On the day before the Communists take over, Quang will fly his family out to Bangkok. There he already has a small fortune in American dollars in a private bank account. "

She smiled and continued: "Whatever happens in Vietnam, Vu Phan Quang will survive. That was the one thing which you and he had in common, Rene, the very great capacity for survival. When you were lost in the jungle I knew in my heart that you would come back to me, because you are the kind of man who always comes back. And when Vietnam falls to the Communists Vu Phan Quang will survive, because Quang is the kind of man who always survives. I have no fears for him."

Chauvel scowled because she was right and she had denied him his only source of satisfaction. The airliner was now ready for take-off and the warning lights were flashing, and Suzanne leaned over him to fasten his safety belt. She paused before drawing back to fasten her own, and kissed him gently and hopefully on the lips. Chauvel was not prepared to be forgiving yet and he deliberately leaned back and closed his eyes.

When they were airborne Suzanne leaned over him again to unfasten his belt, and again she kissed his mouth. Chauvel opened his eyes and found that she was gazing at him seriously.

"Rene," she said. "I am going to stop taking the pill. When we get back to Paris will you give me a baby?"

Chauvel was caught off balance and he could only blink.

"I would like to have a baby," she explained. "I thought about it often while we were in Vietnam, but there it did not seem right. But now we are going home — "

Chauvel smiled slowly and said:"Suzanne, I will give you two babies, or three, or four! Perhaps that *will* keep you out of mischief!"

He did not really believe it, but it was one solution that he had not yet tried.

******

Far below in the Cholon hospital Mary Francis heard faintly the distant roar of the big Boeing jet lifting itself into the air to begin its homeward flight to the west. She wondered whether Chauvel was safely aboard, for Bill Harvey had appeared at the hospital earlier that morning to tell her briefly what was happening and to give her the keys of the little Renault saloon which Chauvel had left to her as a parting gift. She knew that he was not fit to travel and she was still worried about his condition.

The baby in her arms moved and gurgled impatiently, and brought her attention back to the task in hand. She was holding Phat Sang's baby in the cradle of her left arm, and the teat of the warmed milk bottle she was holding had slipped from its mouth. She inserted the teat again and the baby sucked happily and looked up at her with bright, narrow little eyes. Mary smiled down at the infant, and wondered what would happen to it when she too was obliged to leave Vietnam. The little girl's life had been

234

saved, but already she was an orphan and already the little body was marked by the ugly bullet scar that was her birthmark streaked across her left hip. The child was half American and half-Vietnamese, a half-caste bastard with no home and no future and no hope, symbolic of the country of Vietnam itself. Mary wondered what had been the point of saving its tiny life, and there was no answer except that it would have been even more difficult to let it die.

She finished feeding the little girl, and then placed her back in her cot. The baby lay still and watched her and Mary smiled again before she went back to her work. There were more lives to be saved, and more sick to be healed, and more babies to be fed, and that was her role in the vast, writhing, multi-colored kaleidoscope of conflict that was life. A woman had just been admitted with leprosy and there was no cure except to amputate her afflicted arm. The sun was shining and Thi Xin was dreaming of her coming wedding to the handsome young intern Doctor Ton Thu. The lavatory was blocked again and the number of plague victims was increasing.

GALACTIC PROBE; ONE-ZERO-FIVE
LOCATION: OUTER SOLAR ORBIT
PROBE DATE 185/742

The observation capsule was slowly drawn into one of the lower docking bays of the huge, elliptical Timeship, and the long-range extractor beam that had plucked it gently from earth orbit was de-activated. As the power faded and the capsule came to rest the outer vacuum-lock doors rotated to close, shrinking and then shutting out the last glimpse of the earth star and Pluto's rim. After a short delay the docking bay flooded, the inner hull doors opened and the water pressure was equalized. The capsule hatch opened and Jarhl and Korhl were free to swim out into the welcoming ocean of the Timeship. Their long surveillance was over. They were home.

They were now six minds in four bodies. Jarhl Three had left Phat Sang in the last few moments before her death. Jarhl-Two, Korhl-Two and Korhl-Three had remained with their respective human hosts until the last possible moment before the capsule had been withdrawn. Immediately the Korhl triad had been reunited they had separated again, but this time into three dividing Marregh bodies - it was the natural Marregh way of reproduction The three minds of Jarhl knew that their time to complete the current cycle was long overdue, but the triad was still stubbornly resisting division. There was one task left for the united tri-mind to attempt.

The three small, single mind units emerged first, with the larger bulk of Jarhl following more slowly, and with some pain. Revehl and Mirehl waited to greet them, and behind them was the vast shoal of the lesser tri-minds, a thousand bobbing, trailing shadows in the half-lit steel depths.

Waves of pulsed mind warmth engulfed them. They were embraced in pure mental joy, honored and applauded for their long and total dedication to their mission. All minds melted to celebrate their home-coming.

When the rapture was over the mass mind-melt slowly disengaged. There was an uncertain pause and then Jarhl moved physically closer to confront and petition the elders. He/they mind-pulsed the painful question:

"Is the decision still to exercise the Tarlus Precedent?"

The dissention had been expected, and now there was mind silence except for Revehl's regretful affirmative.

"I/we protest this decision. I/we believe it is wrong."

"All the objections were carefully examined and presented by your ancestor Jarehl before his decease. There is no more to consider."

Jarhl quivered in agitation. "I/we feel that we must endorse Jarehl's counsel. We believe that there is more to consider."

Mirehl made a disparaging mental groan.

Revehl mind-sighed.

"Very well," they conceded.

"We will listen."

The Jarhl triad gathered their thought. Jarhl-One amplified it: "The last stages of our mind-melts have shown us that human concern for each other can rise above their basic aggressive instincts. The almost total unselfishness of Mary Francis and her colleagues at the Cholon hospital have been shining examples. Also we have seen throughout our study that Rene Chauvel has tried to reveal the truth and folly of Vietnam to his world, and although his efforts seem to have been in vain, we must give him - and others like him - the credit for trying. Even the arch-fiend, Vu Phan Quang, in the final analysis, chose to save the life of his enemy."

"Quang acted, as always, out of self-interest. Suzanne Chauvel had threatened to kill him if he murdered her husband."

"Quang was too powerful to truly fear her threat. He chose not to start a course of action that would harm her."

The elders contemplated. The shoal hummed with small mind flashes and flickers of mental activity, but there was no forceful interruption. Finally Revehl communicated again.

"Jarhl, we understand your empathy and your concern with these humans with whom you have been so intimate. We commend it. But the horrors we have seen through the minds of Nguyen Nam Kirn and Irvin Jones - the moral blindness and the unthinking aggression of the human species as a whole - has far outweighed anything good and hopeful that we have found. Our conclusion still remains that these creatures are far too dangerous to be left unchecked."

"Then consider this, our legend of the Universal Mind." Jarhl drew upon the memories and knowledge of Jarehl, which he had memorized in turn. "We know that all intelligence throughout the galaxy has formed the hypothesis that there is something, either Being, Mind or Spirit, which is infinite -- which has created and maintained all structures of existence. We must ask why is this God-hypothesis so persistent? Why does it appear with all known cultures, societies and life forms? One possible answer is that the hypothesis does reflect an awareness of something indefinable, but real, and existing in all existence. I/we say that we dare not neglect this possibility, for it may be that there is a Being/Mind/Spirit, which in the fullness of time will sit in ultimate judgment upon the Marregh/Riken, just as we have sat in judgment on the humans of Earth."

Mirehl answered patiently. "We have examined these issues in great depth with Jarehl. There is nothing to show that this hypothesis/belief is anything other than subjective to each individual life form. There is no evidence that this recurring phenomenon is anything other than a combination of imagination and need-fulfillment. In all our time of existence, and through all our explorations of the galaxy, the hypothesis has never been proved. There has never been any objective evidence that it reflects any form of reality."

"Then the hypothesis is so far unproven - it has not been proved false."

Mirehl's mind flashed irritation. There was no rational answer to impasse and stubbornness.

Jarhl could feel his body-strength and mind powers draining. The need to divide was pulling him apart. He gathered all his failing resources for one last effort and launched his final argument.

"Then consider this also - If the Marregh/Riken destroys the humans of Earth because we feel threatened by them, then we shall be acting on the same aggression level as the humans themselves. Our action as a race will be that of one race attacking another because we believe the other to be a danger to our own survival. This is the behavior motivation/mode of human beings when one nation attacks another, or when one human individual attacks another. We shall display exactly the same loathsome self-interest and aggression that we have seen so often in Vu Phan Quang. The Marregh/Riken, as a race, will have proved itself to be no better than a corrupt earth politician."

Now the shoal made itself heard. There was a chorus of mind protest, division and uncertainty. The elders concentrated, absorbed and tried to shape order. Jarhl had shocked them, and now there were currents of uncertainty and doubt.

Jarhl felt some satisfaction, but also anguish because he could do no more. He was beginning to come apart. He was no longer one but three as his mind brothers slid away in what were now three separate body vehicles. There was something exquisite in the anguish, a deep joy of fulfillment in the blissful pain. And then he was one again, but one diminished. Jarhl-Two and Jarhl-Three would from now on maintain their individual existence. As division took place the shoal engulfed them, all minds loving and supporting, sharing in the pleasure and wonder of the new births.

******

After a while Revehl and Mirehl drew aside from the celebration to commune quietly together. Jarhl's last unified observation, and the general reactions, had left the two elders troubled. To see themselves on the same immoral level as the species they intended to erase from the galaxy was indeed to see the issues in a new light of revelation. And the perception was most uncomfortable. The mind pulses that flickered between them were tinged with distress and consternation.

The thought beam from Galactic Probe One-Zero-Seven, amplified by Voronh, the brother ship's Prime Focus, bathed them in consolation. It probed like a shaft of sunlight through the clouds of misgiving.

"We understand your dilemma. Like you we feel a reluctance to exercise the sanction we have been given. There are differences between Earth and Tarlus. The earthlings are not yet as technologically advanced as the Tarls. There is still time for further consideration."

Revehl hesitated. Around him there was no fixed or clear pattern of response which he could coordinate and amplify. He mind-pulsed through space alone:

"What is your counsel?"

"That we should remain here, while your ship makes the star-leap back to Rike to engage the full wisdom of the race. While we act as your beacon, One-Zero-Five will have no difficulty in locking on to our position in order to return to these precise space/time coordinates."

"And in the meantime, if the humans should discover and attack your Timeship?"

"Then we will exercise the Tarlus Precedent. We all know what you know. If it becomes necessary before your return, we will act."

Revehl registered a majority of assent from his fellow Marregh. Mirehl pulsed a faint flicker of objection, but then let it subside. Revehl experienced relief and flashed acceptance:

"So be it. We will act on your counsel."

******

When the Timeship disappeared it was as though a pebble had been thrown into its reflection in the black pool of space. The ship's outline shimmered, distorted, and then dissolved into streaks of horizontal light. Then, like an invisible blind being drawn, the lines of brilliance narrowed and were squeezed out of existence. The star systems that had been obscured before now gleamed bright and cheerful in the far heavens

.Galactic Probe One-Zero-Five had gone.

Galactic Probe One-Zero Seven remained.

The fate of humanity had been deferred.

For a year?

Or a decade?

Perhaps a century?

But, unless there was some reformation of the human character, only until the Marregh/Riken returned. Until then the future of the human race would remain balanced on extinction's edge.

ABOUT THE AUTHOR

Robert Leader has written more than 70 books, including crime thrillers, espionage and high adventure novels, horror and heroic fantasy.

THE SWORD LORD, SWORD EMPIRE and SWORD DESTINY form THE FIFTH PLANET trilogy set in the Earth solar system before the last ice age. These three books are published by Samhain Publishing at www.samhainpublishing.com

SEASCREAM and WITCHFIRE, the latest horror novels are published by Solstice publishing at www.solsticepublishing.com.

Robert has his own website at www.robertleader.com which showcases a full biography and a lifetime of travel and written work. Here you will find introductory FREE books and more low cost e-books. Robert has also published over 200 magazine articles, four souvenir guides to the English counties of Suffolk, Norfolk, Cambridgeshire and Essex, all illustrated with thousands of his own photographs.

BLOODY BURY ST EDMUNDS and EXPLORING HISTORICAL ESSEX are both published by The History Press at www.thehistorypress.co.uk IN SEARCH OF SECRET SUFFOLK and INSEARCH OF SECRET NORFOLK are both published by

Thorogood publishing at www.thorogoodpublishing.co.uk

The Robert Leader website is designed to be of continuing interest to both readers and writers. The stories behind the stories will explain how the books were inspired and created, and it is intended that many more of Robert's currently out of print novels, plus more new novels, will be regularly added to the new e-book list. www.robertleader.com is a site that will repay many repeated visits by anyone who is interested in books and the craft of writing.

THE FIFTH PLANET

BOOK ONE

THE SWORD LORD

BY ROBERT LEADER

They came from Dooma, the fifth planet in the solar system, a planet destined to destroy itself in the holocaust war between the two great continents of Alpha and Ghedda. They came in separate expeditions, each one seeking a potential refuge on the third planet, the only other inhabitable planet in the solar system.

They came in the dawn of time, when the Earth was young, to discover an ancient India, where the splendid kingdom of Karakhor was locked in its own deathly struggle with the massed forces of Maghalla and their allies of sub-human tribes.

And so began the tragic double love story; of Kananda, the First Prince of Golden Karakhor, for Zela, his beautiful golden-haired Alphan Goddess from the Stars -- and of his sister Maryam, the wild rebellious princess of Karakhor, who was fated to love, and be loved, by Raven, the ruthless, blue-skinned Sword Lord of Ghedda.

From the exotic mists of Vedic mythology, to the harsh and barbaric Gheddan Empire, where the law of the Sword is carried godlessly into the space age -- and back again to the great climatic war of the *Mahabarata,* THE FIFTH PLANET chronicles the last desperate days of one world, and the grim, blood-stained beginnings of another.

THE FIFTH PLANET
BOOK TWO
SWORD EMPIRE
BY ROBERT LEADER

The first Gheddan mission to control the Third Planet has failed. The Sword Lord Raven has been driven out of the ancient Hindu Kingdom of Karakhor and forced to return to Dooma. He takes with him Maryam, princess of Karakhor, who sees him as her lover, and a possible saviour in the coming battle against the might of Maghalla.

They are pursued by Kananda, First Prince of Karakhor, drawn by his love for Zela, and his determination to find the sister he believes has been taken by force.

On the Fifth Planet they are all hurled into the terrible arms race between the warring continents of Alpha and Geddha. A planetary cataclysm looms as Kananda and Zela undertake a desperate mission into the heart of the Sword Empire. For Zela it is a race against time to save her world. For Kananda it is a matter of love and honour to find Maryam. And both of them are seeking vengeance against the Sword Lord.

THE FIFTH PLANET
BOOK THREE
SWORD DESTINY
BY ROBERT LEADER

On the Third Planet the Great War with Maghalla has begun. The ancient Hindu Kingdom of Karakhor is under siege and facing its darkest hour. On the Fifth Planet the insane arms race between the continents of Alpha and Ghedda has come to its catastrophic conclusion. Earth is now the only inhabitable planet in the solar system.

For Kananda, First Prince of Karakhor, and his sister the Princess Maryam, their homecomings are a mixture of pain and grief. For their lovers, Zela, Space Commander of Alpha, and Raven, the last Sword Lord of Ghedda, this final refuge is where they at last come face to face.

Here, on the blood-soaked battlefield, is where Zela demands her vengeance, and where Kananda must challenge Sardar the Merciless, the dread King of Maghalla.

All three books of THE FIFTH PLANET are published by www.samhainpublishing.com

BOOK ONE OF THE BRAND NEW
THIRD PLANET TRILOGY
THE GODS OF ICE
BY ROBERT LEADER

The Fifth Planet has been destroyed in the Holocaust War, and now the fate of Earth, The Third Planet, rests with Raven, the last Sword Lord of Ghedda.

A gigantic fragment has broken away from the new asteroid belt formed by the destruction of the fifth planet and is on a collision course with Earth's moon. The impact will push the moon into a decaying orbit which will destroy the last life-bearing planet in the solar system. Raven's space ship can be repaired by cannibalizing parts of Zela's crashed space ship, but it will take Raven and Zela together to fly it on one last mission to deflect the asteroid.

However, Raven has gone into exile with Maryam. Kananda and Zela, now King and Queen of Karakhor, set out to find them.

Their twin journeys take them across Earth as it was between the last two ice ages. The continent of Antarctica is slowly drifting south, the north side of the continent is still habitable but the ice wall is advancing as the whole continent moves into the South Pole.

The wanderings of Raven and Maryam lead them to the Tar Tikans, a mysterious race of benevolent teachers. The Tar Tikans are the survivors of a crashed space craft from Orion. The indigenous inhabitants of Antarctica are the Jiptors, creators of an embryo civilization which will eventually be forced to move from their own Nile Valley on Antarctica to the New Nile Valley in Africa.

In what is now Central America, the first blood-stained kingdoms of the Maytecs has also appeared. The teachers are trying to guide all these emerging peoples but Chac Mouel, the teacher entrusted with the development of the Maytecs is also the reincarnation of Strang, the first Gheddan Sword Lord, who died five hundred years before. Strang is determined to recreate a new Gheddan empire and to destroy the Tar Tikans who would hold him in check. He is an astral traveler with terrible powers of mental coercion.

THE GODS OF ICE is published as an e-book by Kindle Direct Publishing and as a print book by Amazon Create Space Publishing.

THE HORROR NOVELS
BY ROBERT LEADER
WRITING AS ROBERT CHARLES

WITCHFIRE
BY ROBERT CHARLES

The sensational press called it the Breckland Triangle, the three cornered area of Breckland where in the short space of a few weeks the outbreak of serious fire incidents soared out of all normal proportions.

Houses, factories and crashed vehicles burst into infernos of flame. The toll mounted, often from what seemed to be some inexplicable form of internal human combustion. In the skies above the jet fighters from the nearby USAF Air Base pose the constant threat of a major disaster.

Is the new and bitterly opposed toxic waste plant somehow responsible, contaminating the air with an invisible poison?

Or is there something more sinister, a more ancient force of evil stalking the dark Breckland forests?

Perhaps the key to the mystery lies in dreams, in the wild tormented nightmares of a once great monastery sacked by a howling mob, of Satanic orgies at the blood-soaked Druid's Altar, and the curse of a beautiful witch wreathed in flames.

SEASCREAM
BY ROBERT CHARLES

It was out there somewhere offshore in the thick swirling mist which filled the pitch black night.

It was a diffused sound which could have come from any direction, or from all directions

AS THOUGH THE SEA ITSELF WAS SCREAMING

The sea creatures were not unknown. They were frequently sighted and recorded in the days of sail when ships moved silently under wind power, or lay becalmed in remote parts of the world's vast oceans. The sightings stopped when the ships were fitted with noisy thudding engines and kept to direct but relatively narrow sea lanes which the creatures learned to avoid.

But the creatures were still there, far down in the abyss depths, where they might have remained, unseen and undisturbed, if Aztec Three had not exploded to turn the sea above them into a sea of fire.

The creatures moved east across the Atlantic. They were angry and they were hungry, and for those who had to live and work upon the sea it was the beginning of a savage, screaming nightmare.

WITCHFIRE and SEASCREAM
are both published by
www.Solsticepublishing.com

A BRAND NEW THRILLER

SERPENTS IN EDEN
BY ROBERT LEADER

THEY WERE SHIP-WRECKED IN PARADISE
BUT PARADISE HID A TERRIBLE SECRET

A romantic second honeymoon cruising around the paradise islands of the South pacific had seemed the perfect cure for a failing marriage. But for Nicola and Greg Conway it hadn't worked and a freak storm and sudden shipwreck with enigmatic skipper Jack Baker was not part of their plan.

They were washed up on to a tropical island occupied by a small religious community. The Children of New Eden lived a seemingly idyllic existence but were shrouded in mystery.

Why had the cult fled from California, and why was the small community graveyard filled with a disproportionate number of little girls.

Soon Nicola begins to wonder if their presence here was entirely by chance, for it seems that Jack Baker has his own agenda.

As the tensions heighten and the mysteries deepen the malevolent presence of an ancient stone idol watches over them from a forbidden cliff top temple site high above the beach.

SERPENTS IN EDEN is published as an e-book by Kindle Direct Publishing and as a print book by Amazon Create Space Publishing.

More information, the stories behind the stories and free read extracts from all the books, plus free read book downloads, can all be found at Robert Leader's website.

www.robertleader.com

Printed in Great Britain
by Amazon